D1131934

# The Grommets:
## The Secret of Turtle Cave

The following story is fiction. The characters are fictional and any resemblance to any event or person alive or deceased is purely coincidental.

Visit www.booksurge.com to order additional copies.

# MARK-ROBERT BLUEMEL

# THE GROMMETS

## THE SECRET OF TURTLE CAVE

2007

# The Grommets:
## The Secret of Turtle Cave

*This Book Is Dedicated To My Hero, Todd Rundgren, "The Individualist." His Music Has Been A Source Of Inspiration, Comfort And Healing For Me, Since I Was A Grommet. Go Ahead And Give Him A Listen, But Don't Just Stop After One Song Or Album… Todd's Music Is Like Riding A Wave; Unpredictable, Fun, Challenging, And Spiritually Cleansing.*
*Visit Todd At www.patronet.com!*

# INTRODUCTION

This is my first book. I would like to thank my wife Michaelle, for all of her love, help and support. To Nancy Bernal Sirot, thanks for being a friend and creating all of the art and illustrations, you rock! Also, I would like to send a big MAHALO to my home-girl, Shannon Lucier, at monstergraphics.net; for her help with the graphics. Without the encouragement of my family and friends, this book would not have been possible. It would be impossible to thank all of you individually, but you know who you are. THANKS! As far as cave exploring and surfing in areas where there are no lifeguards, this is book is fiction, DON'T DO IT! Always be safe, have fun, and be kind! You can learn more about The Grommets and surfing at www.TheGrommets.com.

# CHAPTER ONE
## Dawn Patrol Rescue

SHHHHHH! I have to keep the noise level down. It's 5:30 a.m. I'm meeting Jimbo and Oz to go surfing. They are my best friends, and we always surf together every chance we get. We are going on a 'dawn patrol' which is what we call surfing at sunrise. Shark experts advise against it, but the early morning is the best time to surf. The waves are glassy and the wind is usually calm. Most importantly, it is never really crowded since everyone is still asleep.

A true dawn patrol means surfing while it's still dark, before the sun even begins to illuminate the sky. You really have to love the sport to wake up before morning and jump into chilly water. It's a lot easier in the summer when it's warm. The buzzing of the alarm sounds like it's nagging you in your sleep. You wonder if you are crazy, getting up at this time to jump into the bitter water, but once you feel the joy of catching your first wave as the sun is peeking over the horizon, you know you are very sane. Then, you are stoked you did it!

Even now as adults whenever we can, Jimbo, Oz and I meet and go surfing before sunrise, especially during the summer months. Many years ago when we were kids, one eventful dawn patrol really shaped our surfing lifestyle. The sky was overcast. The rising fireball hadn't burned its way through the cloud layer yet, but I still rubbed a generous amount of sunscreen on my pale skin. My mom used to yell at me if I forgot. She always worried that I'd get skin cancer like my grandfather. He had a mole surgically removed from his nose, and the dermatologist blamed the cancer on our Nordic, Germanic heritage and the fact that he never applied sunscreen in his life. Oz is much more fortunate because he has dark skin. His parents came here from Peru when he was a baby. Jimbo and I get sun burned a lot easier than Oz. Actually, Jimbo doesn't tan. His freckles just get bigger.

Anyway, the three of us walked past the lifeguard tower down to the shoreline. My feet felt the coolness of the salt water. I was glad to be wearing my cozy wetsuit. We waded into the murky brine until the water reached our knees, then jumped on our surfboards, and paddled out into the lineup of incoming waves.

As I pushed through the first rush of white water, the blast of the cold sea awoke my senses in an instant. After paddling out about fifty feet, we halted in a spot where the waves were beginning to break. Two other surfers were in the lineup about thirty feet north of us. We hunkered on our boards floating silently in the windless air. The sun rose, illuminating the heavens through the clouds with an orange and red explosion.

Within moments, the first set of waves rolled toward us. Jimbo paddled past me to get in a better position to catch a ride. Oz was already at the peak of the first wave. He turned his surfboard around and pushed it back into the wave's face, with both hands gripping the rail. When Oz's surfboard popped back out of the water, it took only two quick arm strokes for him to catch the first morning swell. As he hopped to his feet, he glided over the wave's smooth glassy face and vanished out of our sight.

Jimbo suddenly caught the second roller. I was too far out of position for it and waited, until a gray wall of water rose behind me. My arms paddled frantically, propelling me with all my might. Suddenly, I felt the intense jerk of the surge sucking my surfboard into the wave. I instantly jumped up and planted my feet firmly on the deck of my board. Now, I was free-falling down a glassy wall of water, feeling instant joy! At the bottom of the wave, I cut a sharp right turn. With my arms outstretched like wings, I glided through a steep section of the cool sea, turned, and shot the nose of my surfboard up to the lip of the cresting wave. Glued to the deck, I emerged halfway out of the water on the pinnacle's face. Pushing my back foot down, I whipped my left shoulder behind my upper body, triggering a full 180-degree left turn. My board spun around and plummeted back down the face of the breaker, gaining velocity as I skimmed over the ocean's surface. Racing through the next section of liquid wall, my speed increased. Within a split second the wave burst apart and collapsed on top of me. POW! The rush of water knocked me off my surfboard. Before splashing down, I noticed Oz propped up on his stick staring straight at me. I tumbled headfirst from the peak of the wave into the chilly water. A hollow tube of turbulent ocean wrapped itself around me. My body spiraled under the sea until the force of its current had passed. When I was released from its suction, I headed up for air. After breaking through the ocean's surface, I shook the water out of my hair and rubbed the burning salt out of my eyes.

"That was classic!" Oz greeted me with a hoot.

"Did you realize you had a tube behind you?" He chuckled at my missed opportunity.

"Yeah," I replied sheepishly and got back on my board. "But I couldn't resist banking that last turn. Next time I'll pull it off!" I proclaimed out of breath.

"I've got to get out there and repeat your heroics!" Oz sounded the battle cry as he began to paddle full speed back out to the lineup where Jimbo was waiting for us. I quickly followed him.

We reached our destination just in time for the next set of waves. Jimbo again caught the first ride. Oz paddled a little further out and got the next one. I tried to catch the following wave, but it crumbled and closed out around me.

The sea floor at Main Beach is smooth and sandy. As the sand shifts, the waves will often break in different places. Reef or rocky breaks are usually consistent once you become familiar with the spot, and you can almost tell with certainty where the next wave will break. When the bottom is sandy, sometimes it's a gamble where the best place to take off is.

After riding their chosen waves all the way to the shore, Oz and Jimbo began their long paddle back to me in the lineup. I glanced at my friends and then turned my gaze to the horizon eager for the next set of waves. Looking out over the sea, I saw something peculiar and pale bobbing farther south of me. I stretched my body up to secure a better look. I was certain it wasn't a buoy or a bird.

My eyes focused on the head of a lady wearing a white bathing cap. It is not unusual for people to do their early morning swim at this beach. The swimmer was about one-hundred feet away from me, splashing awkwardly. No one else was in the water nearby. The milky cap disappeared, and then reappeared. Her arms were flailing weakly in the water. It was obvious something was definitely wrong. The swimmer's head went down again. I turned around and searched for my friends. They were at least fifty feet away, but when another set of waves hit the shallower water, I lost sight of them. I heard a piercing scream. The woman was drowning! I began paddling as fast as

I could; lowering my head to reduce the water resistance on my surfboard, which in turn increased my speed.

The white head disappeared out of view. I could hear the elderly lady's faint cries for help as I paddled closer. Her head vanished below the water again, and all I could see were her wrinkled arms like two poles rising out of the water. The lady's head popped up. I saw terror in her eyes as she let out an abysmal groan.

"Grab my surfboard," I yelled as I slid off the waxy deck and pushed it toward the lady. Her left arm slapped the board's deck, and then she hugged it tightly with both hands. The woman took a large gulp of air, then exhaled and inhaled repeatedly. It took several moments before she caught her breath, and I was finally able to relax a little.

"Thank you! Thank you! Thank you!" The lady cried.

"I have cramps in both of my legs." She paused and took a deep breath. "I can't swim anymore. You saved my life, young man."

I watched as my friends paddled towards us at a frenzied pace.

"Just keep holding onto my surfboard, Ma'am." I instructed her as I secured the edge of my board to keep it stable. She continued to bear hug the plank with all her might.

My wetsuit allowed me to float in the ocean with ease next to her. When you aren't accustomed to it, a surfboard is very wobbly and not easy to stand on or sit on, especially a short stick like mine. Kicking my feet while treading in the water with my free arm, I was able to stabilize the surfboard to prevent it from flipping over.

They finally reached us.

"How's it going?" Oz asked, looking concerned.

"We're pretty far away from the shore!" Jimbo was out of breath.

"Are you okay, lady?" Oz inquired, and shot me a questioning glance. I nodded at him confidently.

"You have some seaweed on your face," Jimbo gently peeled it away.

"Seaweed's the least of my problems right now." The lady panted. The frightened woman was still clinging to my surfboard. "Thank you, boys," she said and took several more deep breaths. She struggled as she told her story.

"I developed a cramp in my left leg and decided to swim back to the beach." Her eyes darted back and forth. "But, the harder I tried to reach the shore; the more I seemed to drift further out to sea. My legs cramped up. I was almost ready to give up when your friend here rescued me. Thank you so much!"

"Don't worry, we'll get you to shore safely, Ma'am." I assured her.

"How?" Jimbo asked with a tinge of doubt, his eyes focusing on the waves we'd have to pass through.

"We're gonna stay together and start paddling as fast as we can back to the beach!" I commanded.

"Look! Here come the lifeguards!" Oz shouted, pointing to the shoreline.

The lifeguards rushed out in their red inflatable boat. The faint sound of an outboard engine grew louder as they charged toward us.

"They must have spotted the drowning woman from the lifeguard tower by the pier." Oz remarked.

We floated quietly and waited as the rescue boat rapidly approached us, bouncing over the small whitecaps on the ocean's surface. Soon, two tanned lifeguards in red surf trunks and matching wind-breaker jackets were clearly visible. One lifeguard sat in the front of the boat, near the stern. The other lifeguard remained at the rear of the boat where the outboard motor was steering toward our group. The motor lowered its roar when it was about thirty feet from our huddle. The lifeguard in the back of the dinghy turned down the throttle. The skipper rotated the dinghy so that it glided and bowed until the broadside of the boat was within a few yards of us. The lead lifeguard quickly pulled off his wind-breaker, grabbed a red flotation device, and dove into the chilly water. He surfaced next to the lady who was still clinging to my surfboard.

"Is anyone hurt?" The other lifeguard called out.

The woman responded, "I'm fine, now, thanks to these three heroic young men!" Her words gave me a feeling of pride. My face felt flushed in the cool ocean.

Before the lifeguard could speak again, the lady declared sheepishly, "I feel so foolish. I was doing my morning swim and my legs cramped up." As the lady continued on with her story, the lifeguard studied our faces and listened. I nodded when he glanced at me. It seemed that he recognized we had the situation under control.

"It appears that you got caught in a rip current, Madam. Please grab my hand and I'll help you into the rescue dinghy." He spoke in a deep calming voice.

The lady wouldn't loosen her grip on my board.

"Many swimmers don't recognize rip-currents. They encounter trouble when they are captured in the rip-currents, especially at this time of year. Actually, if you had swum sideways, parallel to the shore, and not straight into shore, you would have been able to escape the danger and stroke back to the beach with ease."

The lifeguard introduced himself to the lady as he reached out his hand. "I'm Lieutenant Hale of the City Lifeguard Service, let me help you onboard. Ray Griffin, my partner, will assist you too. Please grab my hand." He patiently repeated.

The woman reluctantly released one arm from the surfboard and grabbed the lifeguard's hand. He placed her palm onto the rope. Her boney wrinkled hand was engulfed by the lifeguard's grip. Oz and I helped boost her into the dinghy as she swung a pale leg over the side. The lifeguard on board pulled her in safely, though not very gracefully.

"In fact," Lieutenant Hale continued, "surfers use rips to get out into the lineup easier. In order to escape a rip current, the main idea is to swim or paddle parallel to the shoreline." He reached out for the lady's wrist, checking her pulse simultaneously while examining his watch.

"You guys want a free ride back to shore?" The other lifeguard offered.

"Sure, if it's free," Jimbo retorted smartly and winked back at Oz and me with a sly grin.

"Okay, it's a deal," Mr. Griffin, the other lifeguard replied.

"Hand me your surfboards and hop in."

"Thanks!" The three of us replied in unison. Mr. Griffin sat at the rear of the boat while the motor idled. He spoke to the lady as he wrapped her in a shiny silver blanket that he had pulled out of a plastic first aid kit. She gripped the corners of the sheet and swaddled it snugly around her shoulders, huddling like a wet puppy on the floor of the rocking rescue craft.

Lt. Hale stacked our boards in the middle of the boat. Oz quickly scrambled in and Jimbo followed with nearly the same ease. I wasn't so graceful. At first, I grabbed the round rubber railing of the boat with my arm. As I attempted to pull myself in, I swung my right leg out of the water and then tried to rotate it around into the dinghy. Suddenly, my arm slipped and I sank back into the ocean. When I resurfaced and cleared the water out of my ears and eyes, I could hear the roaring laughter of my two friends. Both of the lifeguards and even the lady were smiling.

"Whoops," I muttered with humiliation.

"Here let me help you," Lt. Hale grabbed my hand and easily pulled me into the boat with his muscular arms, while I shamefacedly took my seat next to the lady.

"Okay, Mr. Griffin, we're all aboard!" Lt. Hale shouted like a captain on a seafaring ship.

"Aye, aye," his partner responded with a salute, revving the loud outboard motor as he turned the rudder. The stern of the dinghy hoisted out of the ocean as it spun around and dashed back toward the lifeguard station.

Conversation in the boat was impossible due to the sounds of the wind and the thunderous engine. We sat in the middle of the hull, silently enjoying the lift to shore as we bounced over the whitecaps. The sun quickly began to burn through the clouds and the morning haze abruptly vanished. For the first time all morning, I felt the sun's kiss on my face. After our brief journey, Mr. Griffin slowed the engine for the final ten feet. As we reached the shore, the dinghy slid up onto the sand in front of the tower.

"Last stop!" Lt. Hale exclaimed. "I just need to write down your names, addresses, and telephone numbers for our rescue report, gentlemen." Mr. Griffin reached into another plastic box and pulled out a clipboard to jot down our information. He jumped out of the boat and extended his hand to help the woman climb out. She exhaled loudly with a deep sigh of relief as her feet touched the warm powdery marl on the beach.

"I don't know how I'll ever thank you all!" She exclaimed.

The lady gave each of us a hug. After shaking the hands of both lifeguards, and thanking them for the excursion, we grabbed our surfboards and headed down the beach. Walking with silent pride, we basked in the glory of our rescue experience. Unexpectedly, we were brought back to earth with the heckling of an obnoxiously familiar voice.

"Ha, ha, ha! You babies had to be rescued." The voice rudely chanted, breaking our quiet moment of pride.

Straight ahead was Bradley Booker. He planted himself in our path, with a gray football jersey, cut off blue jeans, and black tennis shoes. It was obvious that Bradley had just arrived at the beach and hadn't even been in the water yet. His eyes carried a malicious glare that made me feel fearful. He was a head taller than me, and I was the tallest of all my friends. He stood there for a few seconds staring each of us down to the ground.

I'll never forget the very first time I met Bradley Booker. It was also the first time I ever felt my nose knocked numb after a punch, and my two front teeth were loose for a month. If you look in the dictionary at our old grammar school's library next to the word: 'Bully,' you'll see Bradley's picture there. I'm not kidding either. I first met Bradley last summer while entering Surfside Pizza to play pinball after a long day at the beach. As I reached into my pocket for some change, Bradley pushed me out of the way with his shoulder, forced the quarters from my hand, and started playing the game. The cook tossing pizza's behind the counter saw the whole ordeal and escorted Bradley out. It was a 'hollow victory' though, because he was waiting for me on my way home. He had a crazed look on his face. I got clobbered. The day after he hit me, Oz and Jimbo cut

Bradley's picture out of the school yearbook and glued it into the dictionary. Rumor has it that his picture is still attached to page 187. We never did get into trouble for that stunt. Back then, I always felt nervous around that wicked kid. Now, I just feel sorry for him because he's a big loser.

Bradley approached us. I was only hoping that my friends and I wouldn't have a fight on our hands now. "You geeks had to be rescued! Aw, did you forget your life vests? You guys can't surf, ha, ha, ha." He taunted us as he signaled back to his two older friends who were trying to stand their surfboards up by sticking them in the sand.

Jimbo's face turned salmon pink as he balled his free hand into a fist and shouted at Bradley. "We rescued that lady!" He yelled as he puffed out his chest.

"Don't listen to him, he doesn't know squat," Oz hissed staring at Jimbo sternly.

"Come on," I added.

Jimbo exhaled sharply, then pushed his shoulders back and followed us. Bradley continued his silly laugh, which was soon drowned out by the sound of the waves and the wind blowing onshore. We walked away avoiding a brawl with Bradley and his boys, still feeling proud of the rescue. All of a sudden, I remembered promising my parents I'd lend them a hand around the house.

"Oh no, I forgot that I'm supposed to help my Dad this morning. I'm saving up for a new surfboard and doing extra chores to earn money. I can't wait until I'm paddling on my new stick next spring," I professed out loud. I imagined myself slashing through the faces of huge waves on the surfboard I longed for in the display window at the sport shop in town. "Surfing sure makes working worth it!" I declared.

"Yeah," Jimbo and Oz agreed in unison.

"I'll see you guys later." I hurried home, smiling to myself and daydreaming about the white, swallow tail surfboard with flames airbrushed on the rails and flaring out onto the top of the deck. My dream surfboard was super glossy and I could see the outlines of my reflection on it when I looked at it from the sidewalk window. I rode my bike back home, taking my time to enjoy the crisp smell of the sea. The breeze cooled my wet hair, and my leg muscles felt like they were enjoying the workout. The perfume of the tropical breeze faded while I pedaled closer to my destination, and exhaust from the street traffic consumed my lungs as I traveled farther away from the beach.

Dad, Mom, my little brother Eric and I live in a yellow house with a Spanish tiled roof. We each have our own bedroom. There is a garage for me to store my surfboard, and our huge back yard is shaded by an enormous avocado tree. A massive redwood tree stands rooted on the side of the house outside my window. My bedroom is very customary. Mom lets me hang posters from surf magazines on the walls. I have pretty standard furniture; including a bed, nightstand, and desk. I also have a walk-in closet. The most important part about our house is that it's close to the seashore! We're about three quarters of a mile from the first stretch of sand. At home, there were a million things for me to do. I was industrious the remainder of the day, but it felt great to finish my chores. The next morning at breakfast, my Mom proudly displayed the clipping of a newspaper article from the daily paper. The editorial read:

*"Three local heroes saved a distressed swimmer caught in a dangerous rip current yesterday morning. The rescued woman is a local dignitary."*

The words "local heroes" gave me a sense of pride. The article misspelled my name and went on to explain how we saved the lady. Mom continued to read aloud:

> *"The Axelrods have been living in our city for nearly six decades now. Several years ago Mr. Johannes Sven Axelrod, a famous archeologist, passed away after a long illness. He was survived by his wife Helen. Yesterday during an early morning ocean swim, Mrs. Axelrod was trapped in a rip current that pulled her over a hundred yards out-to-sea. Luckily, she was spotted and rescued by three young surfers nicknamed Buss, Oz, and Jimbo."*

My Mom continued reading and glancing up at me like she was very pleased. Then her eyes watered-up with pride. My mind was elsewhere. 'I hope Bradley Booker sees the article, except he's so jealous, he'll probably never acknowledge that we saved the lady,' I thought.

# CHAPTER 2
## Tube Ride

How 'BIG' is big? When you are talking about waves, what's considered a 'Big Wave' changes from surfer to surfer depending on their physical fitness, endurance, ability, ego, and most importantly their honesty. No matter how great a surfer you are, there will always be breaks that are too gigantic, or otherwise, too dangerous for you to ride. That is one of the beauties of surfing! There are always bigger and better challenges. My first encounter with what I thought at that time were 'BIG' waves happened a few days after we rescued Mrs. Axelrod at Main Beach. On the day we saved her, we rode the first small waves of an approaching monster swell created by a fierce storm that was raging far out in the ocean. In the days after the rescue, the size and force of the breakers increased steadily.

Two days later, watching the TV evening news with my parents, the weather broadcaster reported that there was a huge storm far out to sea that would be sending us waves the next day. She announced:

"...*Wave heights will significantly increase over the next several days and high surf warnings will be in effect over the weekend.*"

I got up from the couch and sat down on the shaggy carpet, my eyes glued to the television.

"*Tomorrow, wave heights will climb between four to six feet...*"

"That means the biggest rollers will be a little taller than me!" I shrieked. My parents eyed me. I realized making that statement in their presence was a huge mistake.

"I don't want you surfing when the waves get big this weekend." My mother spoke firmly. For a moment I froze thinking about the situation really hard. Finally I blurted, "Aw, Mom, that's not going to be for a couple of days. The weather lady said it's only supposed to be four to six feet tomorrow."

My mom turned to my dad. "Honey, speak to your son!"

He sighed and glared at me through the lower part of his reading glasses as he put down his book. "Young man, you know we have a rule that you must never endanger yourself or the safety of others. If you cannot abide by that rule then maybe you do not have the maturity and responsibility to go surfing without an adult supervising you." Dad continued to rant in a firm voice, "Surfing is a sport that involves the unpredictable ocean and certain risks. First and foremost, you must only surf when there is a lifeguard present. In addition, you must be a strong swimmer and always remember to surf with a buddy. That way you significantly cut down any risk of danger. And by danger, I mean drowning!" He finished sternly.

"Okay Dad, you're right," I replied.

He still looked worried but smiled. I didn't mind hearing my dad's lecture for the hundredth time. That night, I dreamed of riding perfect waves.

The next afternoon, I could already hear the faint roar of the waves crashing several blocks away as I rode my bike, board under my arm, down to the beach. I could feel the moisture created by the mist of the breaking waves in the air hitting my face. The waves were huge! Meeting up with Jimbo and Oz at the rusty railing on the top of the stairway at Main Beach, I had a better view. My heart began pounding at the sight of the perfect surf. The sky was a beautiful blue and the ocean's surface was made of black shiny glass. We watched a set of waves rush toward the shore. The first wave peeled off, leaving a wall of water to ride as it zipped to the shore. The line up was crowded with more riders than we'd ever seen at Main Beach. Our jaws dropped as we saw experienced surfers shredding the big waves. A few not so experienced surfers fell off of their boards.

Anxious to hit the water, we raced down the stairs across the sandy beach and dove into the foaming ocean. Naturally, Oz was in the lead. I stuck my toes into the chilly sea. The approaching storm was definitely pushing in colder ocean water. I waded in. When the liquid was up to my waist, I pushed my surfboard in front of me, laid on the deck, and paddled relentlessly toward the outside of the lineup where the waves were cresting. Oz darted twenty feet ahead, and Jimbo was a few board lengths behind me on my left side. You should never paddle directly behind another surfer. If they lose their board, you might get hit hard. The first wall of white water approached Oz. He pushed his board down and disappeared under it. That maneuver's called a duck dive.

When the rush of the wave hit me, I experienced a force much stronger than the usual waves we surfed. It felt like a truck hit me. My surfboard was ripped out of my grip and away from me. The sudden jolt knocked all of the air out of my lungs, as I was pushed down and jostled around under the sea. Tumbling head over heels repeatedly, I felt like I was a rag doll caught in a washing machine. Finally, the tumbling stopped. I was able to open my eyes and orient myself under the ocean. I saw the light glimmering through the surface, and I torpedoed straight up. My lungs were burning and I was frantic for air. Before that day, I had never felt anything so powerful and severe in my entire life. Sure I had wipeouts before, but the intensity of that wave was more than I had ever experienced. Where were these waves coming from? As I burst up through the ocean's face, I took a deep gulp of air. I desperately pulled the leash off my surfboard, and climbed back on the deck as quickly as I could. The impact zone where the rollers were breaking was waiting for me. Oz was farther out and getting ready to duck under the next oncoming wall of white liquid. Jimbo was a few feet to my left paddling towards the outside and into the safety of the deep water. I followed his path.

Waves start their voyage far away before we get to ride them, sometimes traveling thousands of miles through the deep ocean. The energy created by the force and fury of storms and wind pounding on the water's surface far out to sea, translates into sets of waves rolling toward our beaches. As the surf travels uninterrupted across the deep oceans, it becomes more defined until reaching the shallow tidal zone close to shore. When the waves have little depth, they fall tumbling head over heels, breaking near a coast or on a reef. In deeper water, surfers are safe from the most powerful or dangerous part of the wave. I struggled to move away from the impact zone before the next set arrived to pummel me.

Showing no mercy, the next wave pounded me harder than the first one. I used every muscle I had to hold on to the rails of my surfboard, but it wasn't working. The tremendous force of the white water pushed me backwards and ripped my surfboard from my grip again. The energy of the ocean sucked me further underwater. Knowing what was about to happen almost made the experience of getting hit by the next wave worse. I was running out of oxygen and needed to find which way was up real soon.

After what seemed like an eternity under the agitated sea, I resurfaced and grasped a huge gulp of air. I fearfully stared out to the horizon expecting yet another powerful wave to crash on me and 'try to send me home.' I wasn't going to get pounded on again. I quickly scanned the water for my friends. Oz was out of sight but Jimbo was still in view struggling ahead of me as the next roller of the set pushed its way toward us both. My determination was not going to let me give up. Before the rapidly approaching breaker could crash, I dove down to the bottom of the ocean and let my leash do the work, since my duck diving skills were not able to handle these waves. Deep under the brine I was safe, while my board dragged on the ocean's surface getting thrashed upon. I resurfaced and yanked my leash to pull my stick toward me. I paddled out a few more yards, keeping an eye out for the next fearsome wall of water.

The oncoming set of waves was rolling in fast. Again, I abandoned my surfboard and dove deep. My leash stretched like a rubber band, but I was safe underneath the deeper water, out of reach of the powerful force. My body was pulled slightly by the swell's energy, but there was no tumbling. I felt more confident as each roller passed harmlessly over me, while I waited beneath the sea.

About seven dives later, I surfaced again and looked back to the shore. I realized with embarrassment that I had not gotten much further out. The few yards I had gained were lost when the walls of white water pushed me back. Refusing to give up, I paddled more vigorously. I had to get out there.

Finally, there was a calm moment between the sets of great waves. Only smaller sloppy rollers shoved their way to the shore. My arms were burning, and my shoulders, back and neck throbbed from paddling against the stream of currents. I still hadn't caught a ride. Embarrassed and out of breath, my face felt hot. Oz had made it out to the zone and I could see that Jimbo was almost there. I was going to get there too!

Each wave that came through pushed me back a little closer to shore, but I just tried to get on my surfboard faster and paddle harder between each one. My advance was slow, but steady. After twenty minutes, which seemed like hours, I finally met up with my friends near the lineup. I was exhausted, and sat up on my board, now safe in the deeper water. We were just beyond where the waves were beginning to break. The next set became visible on the horizon.

"Nice paddle," Jimbo's face looked beet red from the effort he had exerted getting out there.

"Ha, if you can't get out, you don't belong out." Oz chuckled. He waited for my response. I had none. We watched the older and more experienced surfers catch waves, and slowly moved closer to the spot in the water where the best takeoff was. 'Taking off' is the first maneuver when you jump up on your board and drop down the face of a wave.

Oz lost his patience and began competing for a wave with other surfers. Jimbo and I watched from the safety of deeper water. Suddenly a huge wave rose behind Oz. We could not believe what we were witnessing. The wave grew behind him and he quickly paddled and jumped up on his surfboard gliding down the face of the glassy wall. Two surfers dropped in behind him, but were knocked off of their surfboards by the crashing crest.

"OWWWW!" Jimbo and I hooted in unison.

The top of the wave curled as it broke and Oz disappeared from our sight. Jimbo and I looked at each other and paddled towards the takeoff spot. By now, most of the other surfers had caught their big waves or were pushed into shore after wiping out.

The lineup was suddenly empty, except for Jimbo and me. We sat silently on our surfboards, waiting for the next set. I wanted to catch a big wave too! The first wave rose rapidly. I turned around and began to paddle towards the shore. It escalated behind me and within seconds I felt the surge thrusting me forward. Instantly, I jumped up on my feet, standing up on my board. The sticky wax kept my feet planted firmly on the deck. Dropping down the face of the wave, with my arms stretched out to my sides, I felt like I was soaring through the air like an eagle. I turned right and crouched when, SWOOSH, I was in the tube created by the curling of the wave. It formed a cylinder of ocean encircling me. A silver curtain of water arched over my entire body, as I sped towards the opening at the end of the glistening tunnel.

The roar of the wave filled my head. I held my breath. Time seemed to stop when I was in the tube of that wave. My eyes were glued to the bright sun light at the end of the hollow liquid. Those few seconds seemed like eternity. Finally, a spray of salt water blinded me. Then with a hard shove, I was spit out of the barrel and the wall crumbed behind me. Oz paddled up to me, smiling. His teeth looked bright white against his dark skin.

"Nice barrel, man! You were completely covered by the lip of that wave when it curled, and then it just shot you out! Whew! You disappeared for at least three seconds!"

His final words stunned me, only three seconds? That was strange, it seemed like the ride was a lot longer. If you want to know what it sounds like in side the tube, take a seashell and hold it up to your ear, so like they say 'you can hear the ocean.' Now imagine the sound of the seashell, but amplified a thousand times louder! That's what I heard inside the tube.

The bike ride home was exhausting. I had to stop several times to switch my board from one arm to the other. My legs felt like jelly and my shoulder muscles were burning, but I was glad to have caught the biggest wave. I arrived home just in time for dinner. Mom, Eric and I, ate without Dad. I was so ravenous that I inhaled my meal and then ate a second helping. Surfing really makes me hungry. I'm not allowed to have dessert if I have seconds, but I didn't care, my treat was my very first tube ride.

After dinner, I dragged myself upstairs to my room, and fell backwards on my mattress. Staring up at the surfing posters on the walls around my bed and ceiling, I couldn't help but replay the barrel I had ridden earlier that day like a video in my head.

The ring of the telephone stunned me awake from my sleepy daze.

"I'll get it, Mom." I groaned jumping up from my bed.

"Okay," she yelled from downstairs.

"Hello," I answered the hall phone outside my room.

"Hey, Buzz." Jimbo was excited. "It looks like the waves are going to be huge tomorrow, do you want to go out?" I yawned into the receiver. "You sound half-asleep. Were you dreaming already? Hah! You got worked today, didn't you." Jimbo jeered.

"No, I wasn't sleeping, but if there's a high surf warning posted tomorrow, my parents told me I can't go in the ocean." Was Jimbo going to laugh at me? Surprisingly, he didn't.

"That's okay, we can watch the older guys catch waves. I was really kind of joking anyways. It was scary out there today. Oz said you caught the wave of the day with an awesome tube ride! I totally wiped out on the roller that came right after yours. 'I fully ate my lunch' so to speak." Jimbo laughed and chattered on as if he was talking to himself. Suddenly he stopped. "My mother wants to use the phone. See you tomorrow, Buzz." Jimbo was finished.

"Later." I replied.

I grabbed a book off the shelf and was ready to lie down and read when the doorbell chimed.

"Buzz!" My mom shouted. I dropped my book and slid down the banister adjacent to the staircase toward the foyer entrance.

"Buzz, there's someone here to see you."

Uh-oh, that could only mean trouble, I thought. Who could it be? My buddies were at home. We never had visitors after dinner. I slowly walked into the living room.

The woman we had rescued was sitting on the couch next to my mom. She had my little brother Eric sitting on her lap packaged in his favorite blanket. Mrs. Axelrod was wearing a white dress with brightly colored pink and yellow flowers and a pearl necklace around her neck. She was carrying a big white handbag, which now sat next to her on the couch. Her stature was small, and her petite sandals barely touched the carpet under her feet.

"Buzz, Mrs. Axelrod was telling me how you saved her from drowning yesterday. We read the story in the paper this morning. My husband and I are especially proud of our son." Mom beamed as she spoke.

"Aw, that wasn't such a big deal." I shook the woman's boney hand.

"Young man, I really appreciate what you and your two friends did to help me. I could have easily drowned." The woman had a high pitched voice.

She then opened her handbag and pulled out a small gift-wrapped box.

"I wanted to get you a little something to show you my gratitude," she smiled handing me the package, then pulled a small white handkerchief out of the handbag and wiped a tear from her eye.

"Go ahead and open it," she said as she pushed the box into my hands.

"Thank you, Mrs. Axelrod. You really didn't have to do this," I hesitated and glanced at my mother for permission.

"Go ahead and open it, Honey," Mom encouraged.

"Open, open." Eric giggled.

I tore the paper off and a clear plastic case was revealed. Inside that was a transparent aqua blue watch with a Velcro® wristband.

"Wow!" I was speechless.

"Try it on. It's waterproof, so you can wear it when you go surfing. Do you like it?" The lady eagerly asked.

"Do I ever!" I replied. "This watch is the BEST! It has the tides and moon cycles on it too! This gift is awesome. Thank you, thank you!"

"Now there shouldn't be any more excuses for you returning home late from surfing," Mom winked at me with a grin.

"Thank you." I felt excited looking at the new timepiece on my wrist.

The lady added: "I would like to reward your friends as well. Could you bring them by my house? I have a gift for each of them too."

Just then, we heard noises at the front door. The keys rattled as my dad entered and walked in with his brief case and lunch box in hand.

"Well hello," he greeted us all with a startled look. "There seems to be a party going on here," he added. My mom rose and went over to him.

"This is Mrs. Axelrod." Mom explained. "She is the woman whom Buzz and his friends rescued."

"Oh, please call me Nana," The gray haired lady smiled as my father gently shook her hand. "Your son, Buzz, and his friends are very brave." Nana told my parents about the rescue. I listened proudly.

Then, rising to her feet, she exhaled sharply and said: "Well, I really must be going now. My old dog will be worrying where I am, Poncho's used to getting his dinner right about now."

"Oh please stay," my mom begged.

"Why of course please sit down for a while," Dad encouraged.

"Thank you for the invitation, but duty calls, and I must let you get on with your evening, too. Please don't forget to bring your friends over soon, Buzz. Okay?"

"Sure." I responded.

The lady followed Mom to the front door where they chatted a little while before she left.

"What you did was terrific, I am proud of you son." We continued our conversation in the kitchen as my dad ate his supper. "Your first week of summer sure has been very eventful so far," he said with a smile.

That night, while lying in bed, I gazed at the glow of my new watch. I decided to set the alarm for the last day of summer, seventy-one days left!

# CHAPTER 3
## "What's a Grommet?"

The next morning, Oz was the only one to bring his surfboard to the beach. There was an eerie feeling in the air. Along with the sound of crashing waves, a fine mist drizzled down on us from the towering plumes of ocean spray. We'd have to paddle out a quarter mile from the shore, just to reach the take-off zone. That was the first time I ever heard the deep drone of huge waves exploding their enormous force like a herd of charging elephants. It's a rumbling you never forget, even if you just hear it from shore. A sign was posted: 'CLOSED DUE TO HIGH SURF DANGER.' The beach was officially closed. The white foamy water rushed up over the sand to the sea wall making the beach uninviting, even for the diehard sun worshippers and joggers. The sky was blanketed with a thick gray haze, and the wind carried the foggy mist created by the spray of the huge waves like rain thrashing the shoreline.

Oz was leaning on the railing, overlooking the beach. He nodded when I approached, "Howzit, Buzz?"

"Terrific, Oz. Are you going out?" I questioned. The ocean was murky and foreboding. Main Beach looked like a deserted island.

"Nope, no surfing for me today." Oz looked down at his tennis shoes, "The lifeguards closed the beach, but I saw some guys paddling out. Nobody stopped them. They just walked down and paddled out with really long and narrow surfboards. I trotted after them with my board, but the lifeguards yelled at me through the loudspeaker!"

Just then, Jimbo pulled up on his retro cruiser. He whistled when he saw the enormous waves peeling near the horizon.

"Whew, I guess I wasn't wrong about leaving my board at home!"

"Nope," I replied, "Oz is bummed the lifeguards won't let him surf."

Oz nodded. "Yeah, it stinks."

"Hey look, there are two surfers paddling in!" Jimbo exclaimed. Two little figures could be seen on their surfboards, approaching the beach from about a hundred yards away. They looked like a couple of tiny ants being pummeled by a liquid jackhammer. Further out, another set of monstrous waves loomed toward the outer reef. The first rose and a few little dots of humanity could be recognized desperately paddling out of harm's way. The surfers in the lineup appeared to be microscopic specks from where we were standing on the shore.

"I wish I had a pair of binoculars right now." Oz said and added, "We could zoom in on those guys out there."

"A telescope would even be better. We should chip in and buy one together. I'll bet we could get one at the pawnshop in town." Jimbo piped in.

None of the surfers sitting in the line-up caught that tremendous wave. Instead, they disappeared in a mountain of white water when the breaker crashed on the outer reef. Several other huge waves followed. The walls of liquid thunder pushed forcefully towards the shore. The two surfers we spotted paddling in, caught the white water and rode back to the beach for the remaining fifty yards. They lingered next to each other about ten feet apart. One stayed on his stomach, speeding towards us as he bounced on the rough sea's surface. The other surfer stood up and performed little turns before plopping down on his stomach next to his friend. When they reached the shore, the big-wave riders jumped off their boards and walked clumsily through the wet sand.

"How was it out there?" I asked the men in their black wetsuits as they climbed the stairs where we were standing.

They looked at us and smiled. One of the men laid his ivory board down by the shower at the top of the steps. He tugged at his wetsuit zipper and tore it off his body, before rinsing the sand off under the showers.

His tall and muscular friend pointed at Oz's surfboard leaning on the railing and commented: "That's definitely not the board you want to be riding on a day like today. The waves are nearly fifteen feet, and the faces of the waves are about twenty feet. There is so much water moving around out there, that a little hot dog stick like that won't let you paddle around fast enough to get out or even catch a ride. You need a big wave gun like this, son," he concluded, pointing to his beautiful tangerine colored board. He laid it down on the pavement in front of us. The surfboard looked fluorescent orange under the dull cloudy sky. I studied its shape. It was like a brilliant and impressive sculpture. I had never seen one like it before. We stared it was as if we were admiring a great work of art, hovering around the board in awe.

"Too bad we don't have time to hang around and teach you Grommets how to ride a board like this!" The tall man exclaimed.

The other surfer laughed as he joined us dripping wet with his surfboard under his arm. He turned to his friend who was mesmerized by yet another set of waves rolling in and inquired, "Ready to go?"

The tall man nodded. Picking up his board he said, "Take care, Grommets. Be healthy and stay in shape, and you'll surf the big waves too, someday!"

"Don't forget to eat your veggies." The other teased us.

Both men chuckled as they casually strolled across the parking lot, and then carefully placed their surfboards into the back of a shiny blue pickup truck. They used rolled up towels to cushion the boards and protect them from the rough edge of the truck-bed. The men never lost the serene, strong look in their eyes. They radiated a sense of peace and happiness, and I felt that I wanted to be just like them. Surfing is a very soulful sport. It embodies man's struggle with his own strength and nature, and I hoped that one day, I would possess the skills to surf big waves too.

The tall surfer looked up as if he sensed that we were admiring him. He smiled and waved at us. The men climbed into the cab of the truck, and they drove out of the Main Beach parking lot.

"Later, Grommets!" They shouted at us as they drove by.

"What's a Grommet?" I asked my friends. Jimbo shrugged his shoulders. Oz scrunched his forehead thinking out loud.

"I believe that it's a part used in airplanes," he answered.

"That's weird. Why would they call us airplane parts?" Jimbo questioned.

"I don't know." I said wondering.

Suddenly, it occurred to me that I had forgotten to mention Mrs. Axelrod, 'Nana', and the cool watch she gave to me.

"Hey, I forgot!" I cried out. "The lady we rescued came by my house yesterday. Check this out!" I showed my friends the watch.

"Righteous," Oz admired it.

"Take it off, let me check it out," Jimbo demanded. Pulling the Velcro® strap, I complied, unfastening the watch. He grabbed it off of my wrist and held it in front of his face.

"Awesome! Tides, lunar schedule, and a stopwatch! This is rad!" Then Jimbo put it on his right wrist and said, "We'll need to share this watch since we all saved that lady."

Stunned, I did not speak, but then I remembered to tell them that Mrs. Axelrod asked me to bring them to her house. "Let's go over there now."

"I gotta get my board back home." Oz hesitated.

"Okay, we'll go to your house and drop off your surfboard first." I replied. "You know the overgrown house on Sea Cliff Way? That's where she lives," I added.

"No way!" Jimbo spoke out. "Remember when we were little kids? We used to think that house was haunted and a witch lived there!" I could tell that Jimbo didn't feel right about going.

"We were moron's to believe that stupid neighborhood rumor!" Oz exclaimed.

Jimbo eyed him. "Yeah, and I still wonder." He took the watch off and handed it to Oz, who looked it over and returned it back to me. We unlocked our bikes, and Jimbo and I followed Oz back to his house. He walked into the yard and leaned his board up against the rear fence. We met Oz in the alley behind his garage, so we could store our bikes before walking to Mrs. Axelrod's house.

"I'm not going." Jimbo announced.

"What are you talking about?" I said peering over at Jimbo.

"That place is haunted and you know it." Jimbo kicked a cloud of dirt and raised his arms.

Oz laughed. "Hey, she might look like a witch..."

I interrupted: "She's cool, you guys. Don't be unkind. I'm going because I promised. If you want to follow, fine with me." I started walking away. Jimbo and Oz were arguing for a moment.

"Oops, I forgot to tell you. She said she wanted to reward you guys, too." I continued walking. They quickly followed.

# CHAPTER 4
## The Proposal

You couldn't see very much of Mrs. Axelrod's beach cottage from the street. A huge oak tree, bushes and shrubs hid the view into the property. I really couldn't even tell what color the house was! We approached the front door and had to clear away some ivy climbing up the walls to find the doorbell. I pressed the button once. No answer. We waited. Oz hit the doorbell again.

"Just a minute, please." The elderly lady's voice was drowned out by loud barking. We heard a chain and the clicking of the deadbolt.

"Well, hello! What a pleasant surprise, I'm glad to see you young gentlemen." Mrs. Axelrod greeted us, her snow white hair hung to her waist.

"Hello," I said shaking her wrinkled hand.

"This is Oz, and this is Jimbo," I introduced my friends. Oz shook the lady's hand. Jimbo just stood there gawking at her. I shot him a nasty look, before he finally reached out his hand, too.

"Can I interest you young men in some lemonade? Oh, come in and sit down in the parlor." The three of us walked into the dark hallway and followed the elderly lady into her living room.

"Have a seat on the sofa." She pointed to the couch, and we all sat down.

"I'll be right back with some freshly squeezed lemonade. I'm going to let Poncho out of the bedroom, don't worry about him. He's a rather old and grumpy Rottweiler," she murmured walking back to the hallway.

The house was dark and smelled a little musty. The walls of the living room were covered with photographs in different sized and shaped frames. Most of them were old black and white photos. We heard a door open and then the sound of a slow 'tip tap tip, tap tip tap,' down the hallway. In walked a giant beast, looking more like a bear than a dog, deliberately swaggering his stubby tail back and forth at minimal speed. He walked up to me and paused with his golden eyes glancing at me. I turned my right fist down and cautiously held it in front of the Rottweiler's graying snout. I felt his wet nose and heavy breath on my skin. His tail began wagging a little faster and he put his head on my lap. In dog language that means, 'Hello, friend.'

"That dog likes you." Jimbo broke the silence.

"Do you keep beef jerky in your pocket, Buzz?" Oz asked mockingly.

"Yeah, I don't know why dogs love me so much," I answered, while patting Poncho on the head.

"Maybe it's because you smell!" Jimbo joked. Oz laughed too.

The old dog lifted his head and grunted, thoroughly enjoying the attention. Mrs. Axelrod returned carrying a tray with a pitcher of lemonade, four glasses, and a plate with cookies.

"I hope you like gingersnaps," she said while pouring lemonade into our glasses.

The lady turned to Oz and Jimbo. "I asked your friend Buzz to bring you fellows by so that I could properly thank you for saving me from drowning the other day." She exhaled sharply and sat down in a big wing back chair that stood by a tall, colorful glass beaded brass lamp. Poncho left Jimbo and walked over to the chair and plopped himself down in front of the lady's feet.

Mrs. Axelrod reached into the pocket of her apron and pulled out two small gift wrapped boxes. Jimbo was the first to rip into his package.

"Wow! Thanks, Lady!" Jimbo howled, jumping up and down. He could not contain himself.

"You can call me Nana, please. I went down to the surf shop and they had those watches in the glass display case and I immediately knew that they would be great for you three boys."

Oz received a black watch and Jimbo's was military green. They both put them on immediately. Jimbo left his old watch on, too.

"Thanks! This is the best surprise. We really just did what anyone else would have done in the same situation," Oz said as he embraced Mrs. Axelrod with both arms.

"Oh, Oz, you are such a gentleman. I am very lucky to have met all of you. Are you boys going surfing today?" Nana asked.

"No, the surf is too big." I replied while reaching for another cookie.

Nana turned to Oz and spoke. "That's too bad. I'll bet you are disappointed." She took a sip of her lemonade and continued. "You know, yesterday, I was fortunate enough to meet Buzz's family. What about you Oz, do you have any brothers and sisters?"

"Yes, I have two brothers and two sisters," Oz glanced down at his watch.

Nana then said, "Where are your parents from?"

"Lima, Peru." Oz looked up. "Peru is home to some of the best surfing beaches on Earth!"

"Where's that again?" Jimbo asked.

"South America, you dummy." Oz gave Jimbo a hard look.

Nana smiled and told us about the many times she accompanied her husband on expeditions to South America when they first met. She got up and stood next to Oz.

"I can tell from your dark soul-full eyes, bone structure and jet black hair that you are a descendant of the great Inca civilization. My husband Johannes was an archeologist and we took many trips to Peru." She coughed and took a deep breath. "Johannes took us for several long trips digging in the dirt, searching for artifacts from the ancient Quechuan Empire. We always brought Joey, Clara, and Archibald, our three children. Ah, those were very, very happy times!" Nana exclaimed with a far away look in her eyes. She turned to Jimbo and guessed, "You, on the other hand with your sandy blond hair and freckles lead me to believe that your ancestors may have been from the Emerald Isle."

"I'm Irish, and I don't have any brothers or sisters." He shrugged his shoulders. "Just my mom and I live together." There was a silence in the room. "I never really met my father and don't know much about him." He stared down at the floor.

"I think you'd better start doing your homework, Jimbo." Oz laughed. "Ireland is the Emerald Isle."

"I knew that!" Jimbo smirked as he scratched his head.

"Most of my relatives are from Germany." I joined the conversation.

"I thought you might be of German descent. Your little brother, Eric, looked so adorable in his lederhosen when I dropped by your house." Nana commented. I was embarrassed at the mention of the dreaded leather shorts with the chest-strap suspenders. When I was little, I hated them so much that I peed in them on purpose, I remembered.

"Yeah, my grandparents sent me a new pair from Germany, too, and my parents wanted my brother and me to wear them for our family portrait this year. I refused." I sheepishly admitted. "Unfortunately, Eric thinks it's a Halloween costume and doesn't want to take the lederhosen off." Jimbo started laughing but quickly stopped when I frowned at him.

"Listen boys, I have a proposal for you," Nana pointed out the window into the backyard. "There is a small shack in the rear of my yard. It's completely filled with junk. It was supposed to be a garage but I never have been able park my car in it. If you boys want to clean it out and help me with the yard work around here, I would be willing to let you use it to store your surfing gear or even use it as a meeting place." Nana paused for a moment and continued. We glanced at one another.

"Think about it. I live right at Main Beach. You wouldn't have to carry those heavy surfboards and your wetsuits back and forth all the time." Nana turned toward us and smiled, offering each of us another cookie from the plate.

"I wouldn't charge you rent for using the shack if you could help me handle this yard. I'm afraid I've let it grow into a jungle. I simply can't landscape it myself, and I certainly cannot afford a maintenance worker on my fixed income. Of course you must ask your parents first, but what do you think?" She asked.

"That sounds great," I thought aloud. "It looks like a clubhouse."

"Awesome!" exclaimed Jimbo as he pressed his face against the window for a better look at the shack in the back yard.

"Yeah!" Oz beamed looking over Jimbo's shoulder.

"Why don't you go out and take a look," Nana suggested. Jimbo shoved another cookie in his mouth as we got up from the sofa. Poncho remained glued to the rug in front of Nana's chair. As we followed her through the hallway to the back door of her beach cottage, Jimbo grabbed two more cookies. I shot a disapproving glare his way.

"They were stuck together," he whispered defensively.

Nana opened the back door and led us to the yard. It was overgrown with weeds and a rainbow of wildflowers. The grass was knee high in some areas and a rusty metal clothes dryer stood right in the middle of what was supposed to be the lawn. The fruit trees were overgrown and their untrimmed branches were intertwined with each other. The hedges that surrounded the yard were bushy and tall. No wonder we believed the house was haunted when we were kids.

Nana noticed me staring at her yard with my mouth wide open. "I'm afraid, since my husband passed away several years ago, I've let everything go. My children live far away, so I don't really have family in town, and most of my friends have passed away. It's lonely growing old," Nana handed me an old brass key to the garage. I felt sad for her.

"Wow lady, this is a great idea!" Jimbo hooted. He lived the farthest away from the beach. For him, it was a forty-five minute bicycle ride home after each surf session, compared to about ten for Oz and me. What great luck!

"Call me Nana, it's easier." She patted Jimbo on the shoulder.

"Thanks, Nana," Jimbo was stoked!

I put the old key into the lock and turned it. The door welcomed us into our new hideaway. In the dim light we could see boxes stacked by a window. There were mounds of ragged clothes and antique furniture and other odds and ends.

"I'm sure its going to take us weeks to rummage through all this old stuff." I mentioned.

"I don't care how long it takes." Jimbo ranted excitedly. "We'll turn this garage I into a clubhouse for surfers!"

"Well, with the three of you boys working together, I'm sure you'll have my property cleaned up in no time." Nana continued as she led us to a fence parallel to the alley behind her cottage. "Next time, feel free to use the alleyway out back. It's a short cut."

We walked back to get our bikes at Oz's house, then broke off to go our separate ways.

"Later, Grommets!" I called out to Oz in his yard. Jimbo had already ridden away.

"Tomorrow we'll surf!" I could hear Jimbo holler in the distance.

# CHAPTER 5
## Grounded

The following morning, the usual haze burned off early, and I awoke to a bright blue sky outside my window. I slid on my surf baggies, a ratty old T-shirt, and my new watch. Luckily, my wetsuit was dry. I rolled it up and tossed some surf wax into my backpack too. Dad was upstairs shaving in the bathroom. Mom was already humming in the kitchen making breakfast. I grabbed a banana from the fruit bowl.

"Morning, Mom."

"Good morning, Sweetie. What are your plans for today?"

"I'm going to check out the beach and look for some good waves, Mom."

"Well, I will need you to help watch your brother later," she replied while stirring the scrambled eggs. "Are you hungry?"

"No thanks, Mom."

"Be back by 10 a.m. I need you to take care of your brother while I help our neighbor, Mrs. Watson, so be on time."

"Alright," I shouted running out the door with my gear in hand. I jumped on my bike and headed to the shack. The air was warm and windless. When I arrived at Nana's cottage, Jimbo and Oz already had their wetsuits on.

"Howzit?" I asked.

"The surf is going off! Hurry up, bro. We'll have a session before we start working on the shack." Oz greeted me at full volume. Jimbo nodded appearing impatient and still half asleep. I pushed my bike behind the shack and waved at Nana who was standing at the window by the kitchen sink in her house. She smiled and waved back. After pulling my wetsuit and wax out of my backpack, I grabbed my surfboard and locked the door to the shack before returning to my friends.

"Okay, I'm ready."

We walked down the alley behind Nana's back yard until we crossed the last block to the steps at Main Beach. My heart began thumping faster when I saw the ocean. The waves had dropped a great deal in size since the morning before.

"Perfect waves!" I exclaimed, as we watched the flawless four-foot breakers peeling one after the other.

"OWWWW!" We exchanged hoots at the sight of the surf. Naturally, Oz was the first down the stairs. But Jimbo and I were not far behind. I broke my bar of wax into equal pieces and handed a chunk to Jimbo. We rubbed it on the decks of our boards. Surf wax is a gummy adhesive that keeps surfers from slipping off. Oz attached the Velcro® band of his surf leash to his right ankle. He picked up his board and proceeded to stretch the elastic cord in order to pull out the kinks. That really prevents it from getting tangled up. After I finished waxing, I tossed what was left of the bar to Oz.

"Thanks for saving me some." Oz joked and hastily rubbed wax on two small areas of his surfboard where he places his feet.

On the other hand, I like to have a fresh layer of wax from nose to tail on the deck of my surfboard. Sometimes, having wax on the tip of my board will give me just enough extra grasp to hang on with one hand in a critical situation. As a surfer, one of your main goals is to always maintain control of your stick. We paddled out into the breaking waves. There were only a few other surfers sitting in the ocean further up the beach. This time, I was the first to catch a ride. As the wave approached, I paddled my surfboard as far out and at the last possible moment, spun around real fast and began to advance with all my strength. The rushing sound of the water intensified and I felt the board being pulled forward with a strong jerk. I jumped to my feet swiftly, and experienced the 'free fall' straight to the bottom of the wave. My arms were stretched out like wings. I flew under the crest and turned my board to the right, then crouched down. The wave made a loud WHOOSH. Then I heard a crashing resonance as the wall of water smashed onto the ocean's surface. A curtain of turquoise sea cascaded over my shoulder forming the passageway I was speeding through. I was completely sheltered by the hollow cylinder, and a small opening at the end of its tunnel was all I could see. In an instant, I felt another accelerating push and was blinded by a spray of a clear salty mist. I shook my head to clear my eyes and entered back into the open air. The wave slowed and I was surrounded by its remnants. The wall of white water propelled me towards the shore, and then its energy reshaped itself into a much smaller wave. A feeling of joy rushed through my entire body.

"I got tubed! Wow!" I exclaimed.

With a sharp right turn, I jammed my board up and out of the wave. I plopped back down on my chest and quickly paddled back out toward my friends. As the saltwater ran out of my eyes, my vision cleared just in time to see Oz catching a wave in the lineup. He moved with a solid wide stance, crouching low as the lip of the breaker curled over him. Looking like a statue he disappeared behind the drape of water. I paddled further out towards the lineup where Oz was riding so I could get a closer look. He was only a few yards away. I witnessed my friend squatting low at the end of a deep tunnel of swirling water. In a split second, WHOOSH he was knocked off his board. The last I saw of him were his feet pointed toward the sky—WIPEOUT! You might say Oz was head over heels in that wave. I sat up on my surfboard and waited. Within seconds, Oz broke the surface of the water. He was laughing loudly.

"Did you see that, Buzz? Whew! I was in the Greenroom!" He hooted.

"Yeah, Oz, you definitely were in the tube." I affirmed admiringly.

We paddled out together and Oz babbled non-stop the entire time about his last wave. I listened to my friend, and swiftly increased my momentum, just to keep up with him. In my mind, I was constantly replaying the intense tube ride of that last wave.

Following a fantastic surf session, Jimbo, Oz, and I went back to the shack in Nana's backyard. We leaned our surfboards against the side wall, and took off our wetsuits. We had promised to clean up her yard so we worked for an hour raking, weeding and trimming the shrubs and trees. After we filled four of Nana's trash pails with the loose foliage, we put all the tools back in the garage. Minutes before 10:00 a.m., I bid my friends farewell and raced home to watch my little brother, Eric.

As I rushed into the kitchen my mom was just hanging up the telephone. She looked relieved. "You are here just in time, Buzz. I'm going across the street to help Mrs. Watson now. I'll be home in a few hours. If you need anything just call." She directed as she sauntered out of the room. Mom brought my little brother Eric into the living room and sat him on the carpet in front of me. "Here, this came in the mail today, Buzz." My mom handed me the new super glossy issue of my favorite magazine, Surfer's World. I received the monthly subscription as a Christmas present from my grandparents.

"Cool!" I sunk into the couch, magazine in hand.

"Don't forget to pay attention your brother! I'll play his favorite video. Okay, Eric, I want you to behave for Buzz."

Eric barely glanced up at her, already dancing to the music and the colorful images on the TV screen. Mom gave him a kiss, and turned to me.

"Be good," she commanded as she left the room.

My mom shut the front door, and I immediately buried my face into the magazine. By page ten I had forgotten about Eric and everything else in the world for that matter. I was so exhausted from surfing and doing yard work. I drifted off into a deep sleep.

When I came to, I was surprised. The TV screen was blue and Eric had disappeared. Obviously, I had been asleep for at least an hour—plenty of time for my little sibling to get hurt or in trouble, or worse. I felt a clammy wave of terror cloak my body.

"Oh, no, Eric!" I shouted dropping the magazine as I leapt to my feet, and ran upstairs to my brother's bedroom. I searched his closet, no Eric! My bedroom was empty. The bathroom was empty, too.

"Eric!" I shouted again.

"Where are you? Come out, come out wherever you are." I tried to put on a playful voice to lure him from his hideout. Slowly I pushed open the door to my parents' bedroom, nothing.

"Eric!" I hissed in anger and frustration. Where could he have gone?

"You little butthead," I whispered under my breath.

"The front door!" I thought sliding down the stairway banister toward the foyer. To my horror, I found the door slightly ajar. I began to panic. Was he outside? Thoughts of my little brother being hit by a car or lying hurt in the street flew through my head.

"Eric! Where are you?!" I hollered.

After a minute of frantically searching up and down the street, I rushed into our backyard. He was not there. This was not good. I ran to the garage, both doors were still locked, and looked through the windows. Eric wasn't there either. There was no sign of him, anywhere. I didn't want to call my mom. What would I say? I finally reentered the house through the side kitchen door. There to my surprise, on the floor sat my little brother next to a large silver bowl in a puddle of eggs, flour and milk. The refrigerator was wide open and just about every cereal box from the pantry was thrown to the kitchen floor. Eric was a masterpiece of a mess. His hair and face were powdered with flour. His clothes were blanketed in cereal, in addition to being drenched in eggs and milk. In his sticky left hand, he held a wooden spoon which he occasionally banged on the large metal bowl. I suppressed a giggle. What a sight!

Suddenly, from behind me, I heard my mother clear her throat: "Ahem!"

I froze, feeling her angry breath on the back of my neck. 'Uh-oh,' I thought. I took a deep breath and turned around to face her. My mother had a glare in her eyes that shot right through me.

"What happened in here? I thought I put you in charge of your brother." It was obvious she was straining not to yell at me.

Eric looked up proudly and smiled. "I bake a cereal cake. Want some?" He offered innocently.

"No, Sweetie," my mother's demeanor softened. Mom tiptoed through the disaster area, and retrieved my flour-covered brother. She tried her best to avoid the milk and egg puddles, but that was impossible. Her shoe prints were left in the dusty flour on the kitchen floor.

"Come on, my little baker, you're getting a bath." She held him away from her body to keep from getting more of the mess on her clothes. Before leaving the kitchen she looked down at her sandals, slipped them off as she turned to me and barked, "and YOU," the softness disappeared from her voice. The icy glare returned. "You will clean this mess up now, and I want it SPOTLESS! Then you will ride your bike to the grocery store and replace the flour, eggs, milk, and cereal with your own money. Break into your piggy bank if you must. And by the way, you are grounded for a week. NO TV, NO PHONE, NO FRIENDS, and NO SURFING! You know the drill." Her horrible lecture finally ceased.

Indeed I knew the drill, but her last 'NO' was the most painful. No surfing for a week. I was bummed even more so because it was summertime; but I knew better than to protest. It would be foolish and only increase my penalties.

"Yes, Ma'am." I answered. It always amazed me how my mother could be so sweet to my little brother Eric, then instantaneously transform into a drill sergeant when I did something wrong. Why did I have to doze off?

That evening, I kept quiet at the dinner table. The meatloaf was delicious, but my parents weren't happy about me falling asleep while babysitting Eric. Hearing the same lecture from my dad, with additional commentary from my mom, bugged me even more. Well it couldn't have been worse, I thought.

Due to my punishment, I wouldn't be able to join Jimbo or Oz at the shack. Worse yet, when the phone rang, I heard my dad tell my friends that I was grounded so, no calls either. What was I going to do now? My baby brother smiled at me. Little did he know how much trouble I had gotten myself into, and I had let him down too.

# CHAPTER 6
## The Mysterious Chest

The first day of being grounded seemed like an eternity because I was stuck in my bedroom all day long. Jimbo and Oz came by my house after they had finished working on Nana's yard. My mom was lenient enough to allow me to speak to them for a few minutes at the front door.

"Sorry I can't help you guys work in the yard at Nana's and rearrange the shack."

"Don't worry, we can only work two days this week," Oz assured me.

"Yeah, there'll be plenty of labor left for you." Jimbo piped in. "Oz found a set of bowling pins in that pile of stuff. We're gonna mount them on a plank of wood and make a rack for us to hang our surfboards. Then we'll never have to lug 'em back and forth from home to the beach." Jimbo reported with excitement in his voice.

"Yes, we'll have our own private Surf Headquarters!" Oz shoved his hands into his pockets. "There's a lot of junk that we still have to clear out, and we don't have much space in Nana's trash cans. It will probably take a couple of weeks to complete the job." He continued.

Jimbo interrupted. "Under a pile of old throw rugs, we also found a sofa and a TV-VCR unit that works, so we can watch the surf report and surf videos."

"Hey! We could even save up between the three of us and buy a video camera from the pawn shop and make our own surf movies!" Oz added enthusiastically.

"That will help us shape our surfing style and improve our skills. Maybe we'll even learn some tricks, like a 360 degree turn, or even aerials!" I commented, intrigued by the idea.

After about ten minutes, my mom ended the visit. I was sad that I couldn't hang out with my friends for the entire week. This was going to be a long one. My punishment seemed endless, especially since it was summer and I didn't have school and homework to pass the long days. Eric followed me all around the house. I read books, ran errands with my mom, and did too many chores around the house and yard. After a grueling seven days, my jail sentence was OVER! Freedom and surfing were back.

The first day of liberty came bright and early. Without wasting time, I informed my mom that I was leaving. I grabbed my board and wetsuit, and raced my bike down the street. The wind patted my face. It felt liberating riding again. My first destination was the shack.

It was good to hear the creak of the old wooden gate to Nana's backyard, and to see Jimbo and Oz again. They already had their wetsuits on and were stretching out on the grass, ready to surf.

"You really missed it, Buzz. A couple of days ago the surf was epic!" Jimbo had no problem rubbing it in my face.

My two friends had cleaned out Nana's shack and fixed it up while I was grounded. I admired the work they had done before we went for a surf session at Main Beach. Just as Jimbo had promised, Oz used the bowling pins to construct a surfboard rack. There was space to hang six surfboards.

"How did you do it?" I asked Oz.

"I found seven bowling pins and Nana said we could keep any salvageable junk, so I mounted the bottoms of the pins to the base of the boards with screws."

"It really wasn't difficult to construct once I sketched it on a piece of paper," Oz mentioned as he stood proudly next to his invention.

After the tour, we grabbed our surfboards and headed to a secluded area south of Main Beach. The waves were small and mushy, but it was good to get back in the water after being grounded for a week. We entered the ocean and paddled to a spot that wasn't crowded, and sat there silently waiting for the next set of waves to arrive. On the horizon, I noticed the peaks of approaching waves. I paddled up the shore away from Oz and Jimbo. The water was dark-green and the ocean surface was fairly smooth and glassy. My arms felt rested and brawny as I glided over the water's surface to meet the approaching wave. With perfect timing, I was rewarded with a fun two-foot breaker. It immediately crumbled behind me as I raced up and down the face of it, carving sharp little turns before the entire wave disappeared into the shallow tide.

"That was a killer little curl," I chuckled as I propped myself upright on my surfboard.

"Oh, man! That wave was perfect!" I exclaimed to Jimbo, who was still sitting like a duck where I had last left him. He shot me an envious look and then turned his sour stare towards the horizon.

Another set arrived. Jimbo caught the first wave, but tumbled off. I caught the breaker after that, which was at least a foot bigger than the last racing up and down the face just like on the previous wave. Except that now, with the confidence of my past success I began to cut loose with turns, splashing sprays of water with the wake of my surfboard.

"Owwww!" I hooted as the wave propelled me forward.

That day, my surfing was ON! Sometimes, I feel like I can ride like a pro. Regrettably, there are also those days when the opposite happens, and I feel like I am a beginner surfing like a kook. On those days nothing seems to go right. Jimbo and Oz were still in the lineup when I paddled back from the ride. They eventually started catching waves too, but the good ones were few and infrequent. Today I was the lucky one seizing more than my friends did. After a few more sets came through, the surf was getting weak and the tide changed. As the wind picked up, no more rideable waves were coming through. It was time for me to head home. I didn't want to be late for lunch, and besides, my mom was making fish tacos.

"You guys, I need to go." I told my friends.

"Yeah, these waves stink," replied Oz.

"We're outta here," Jimbo added.

We walked back to Nana's shack, retrieved our bikes, and took off for home.

Later that week, I cruised back to the beach on my bicycle, alone. Oz was visiting his grandparents for the day and Jimbo was babysitting the infamous neighborhood brat. Jimbo was saving up for a new surfboard, too. He was a legend among parents with young kids who required a babysitter in a flash. Even difficult children were no problem. He was the only one tolerant enough to handle Westlyn Junior, the four year-old little monster who would grow up to be a local politician! The surf dropped and after our last session there were no waves for over a week. When there's no surf for more than several days in a row, it's called a flat spell. Unfortunately, we had a major flat spell and the ocean looked like an enormous lake. It was torture!

During a flat-spell, life can become sheer agony for a true surfer. Skateboarding is the next best thing though. Riding a skateboard gives you the feeling of carving turns and if you want, the thrill of going real fast and catching air. But for me, riding the pavement is just not the same as thrashing a wave. We have some friends who love skateboarding and only surf occasionally for fun. We are the exact opposite. My friends and I would rather surf any day!

After we get tired of skateboarding during long summer flat spells, we have to find other things to do. Jimbo, Oz and I swim and snorkel, exploring the ocean cliffs and rocky coast in our area. Jimbo had a spear gun, so the three of us would take turns trying to spear fish with it. Oz brought a float he had constructed out of an old poolside floatation ring and a basketball net, which was tied together at the bottom. He was always prepared in the event that we got lucky, or a fish got unlucky, and ended up on the sharp end of the spear.

On one particularly surf-less day, the ocean was unusually clear. We could see at least fifty feet under water. I drifted away from Jimbo and Oz, who were chasing after a school of long silvery fish. My friends could never get close enough to any fish. The fish always stayed at least ten feet away from the spear gun. Jimbo would try to swim rapidly towards his prey, but they would just glide away with a short burst of speed teasing him. Gracefully kicking my flippers on the water's surface with my arms resting at my side, I scanned the ocean bottom through the frame of my diving mask. Suddenly, there was something dark and square-shaped embedded between tufts of sea-grass on the ocean floor. I took a deep breath through my snorkel and dove down towards the object. The long strands of sea-grass danced back and forth in the tidal surge. A metal chest became visible for seconds and then quickly disappeared from my sight.

As the long stringy grass blades were pushed side to side by the tide, I could see the box clearly. When the current surged back in the other direction it vanished again under an emerald carpet. I wanted to grab it, but the air in my lungs ran out quickly and forced me to return to the ocean's surface. When I floated to the top, I blasted the water out of my snorkel. Was I seeing things?

The underwater surge pulled the tuft of sea-grass to the other side and the square object emerged, and then vanished again. I was about eleven feet below the surface. I took another heaping gulp of air into my lungs, dove down and kicked my fins to propel me to the ocean floor for a closer look. Just as I was about to grab the box, the water reversed direction. Unexpectedly, my facemask was covered by green. The spaghetti-like blades of sea-grass blinded my sight. The fine long strands flipped over my head and I could feel them cascading down my shoulders and back. Despite my desire to stay under water, the air in my lungs made me buoyant. I was forced back up again. When I broke the surface, I exhaled strongly though my snorkel and strained my eyes to find the metal box.

Three more deep breaths later, and after waiting for the sea-grass to uncover the box, I quickly kicked my way back down to the sea floor. Clutching the sides of the chest with both hands, I was disappointed to find it was stuck and would not move. I yanked the box with all my strength. The metal box would still not budge. My lungs ran out of air and the urge to breathe overcame me as I pushed off the sandy bottom and shot toward the surface. After being under water for so long, I didn't have the strength to blow the water out of my snorkel. I urgently ripped it out of my mouth and gasped for air. Back under the sea after a few deep breaths, I watched as Jimbo dove below and pushed over the sea grass. He shot me a curious glance through the glass of his diving mask, and then his eyes lit up. Jimbo gave me the thumbs up sign under water. I took a deep breath through the snorkel and dove toward the chest. My hands grabbed at one side of the box, while Jimbo grabbed at the other and we tugged in unison. With double strength, we felt a slight wiggle. The box was coming loose! But my lungs were burning for oxygen and I lost my grip. Again, I kicked up hard to the surface and tore the snorkel from my mouth. Jimbo followed me.

"What's down there, a lobster? I couldn't tell what the two of you were looking at." Oz inquired, holding the spear gun with the trident head pointing upwards.

"That's a cool box. It looks like some kind of small pirate chest!" Jimbo chattered anxiously after surfacing and ripping the snorkel from his mouth.

"Show me." Oz demanded. He tied the spear gun to the float. Since we hadn't caught any fish, the float contraption had not been tested yet, but for now it was good enough to hold the spear gun while we focused our attention on the mysterious box below.

Oz shoved the snorkel into his mouth, and dove down. I followed. When we reached the floor, I spotted the box right away. Oz watched patiently while I grabbed it and again tried to loosen the box from its place. I could still only get it to wiggle. Then, Oz took charge and clutched the chest with both hands. The three of us surrounded it. Jimbo pulled his diver's knife from the sheath on his calf. He picked at the rocks surrounding the chest, while Oz tried to free it. They both returned to the surface, and it was my turn to dive back down. I saw that they had been more successful. The box was beginning to move. After a couple of turns back and forth, I was able to free it.

"Right on!" I exclaimed as I surfaced and placed our salvaged prize in the net of the float. "Let's get it to the shore and open it up! Hurry you guys, swim faster!" I shouted with excitement.

Kicking his fins hard to keep from sinking, Oz untied the spear gun and handed it to Jimbo. The box was heavy and the ring of the float was weighted down by its mass, just below the water's surface.

"Hey, Oz, let's head towards the beach," I hollered. He nodded. I placed the mouthpiece of my snorkel between my teeth and swam next to Oz who held the box in his contraption. Jimbo followed us with the spear gun in one hand. In the excitement I think we all kicked our fins a little faster than usual. We passed the end of the underwater sea-grass meadow and turned right in front of the rocky outcroppings by the shore. Soon we were over the sandy bottom near the cove. Oz and I reached the beach first, dragging the box in the net with the floatation ring. Exhausted, we laid on the wet sand trying to catch our breath. Jimbo disengaged the spear gun as he approached the beach and propped it up against a rock with the sharp end sticking in the sand. The three of us sat staring at the old metal box while we rested. Our fingers were stained orange and small grains of rust stuck to our hands. The cove was practically deserted except for a young couple reading books and sunning themselves on a blanket.

"Wow, that's an ancient looking box," Jimbo exclaimed!

"Yeah, it looks antique," Oz added, "let me see your knife, Jimbo, maybe I can pry it open."

"Don't ruin the chest," I pleaded with my friend, who only took that as a license to be funny.

"Don't worry," Oz countered, with his eyes crossed. "I know what I'm doing."

"And don't bust my knife, either," Jimbo added.

"Yeah, yeah, don't worry," Oz responded sarcastically and then let out an evil laugh.

Except for scratching the surface of the lock on the box, Oz didn't accomplish anything. I didn't want to complain any more, but I let out a sigh of relief when he admitted that he could not open the box and handed the knife back to Jimbo.

Oz picked up the chest and handed it to me. It was as heavy as a brick. "I give up," he said.

"How will we get it open?" I wondered.

"I could try to smash it open with my dad's tools," Oz added.

"No thanks, I think taking it to a locksmith is a good idea." I said.

Oz hesitated. "I have to go shopping for a suit. There is some wedding that I have to go to."

"I'll meet you at your house at four o'clock this afternoon, Buzz." Jimbo was enthusiastic. "I'll lug your diving gear so you can carry the chest back to the shack," he offered.

"Thanks Jimbo." I handed him my mask, snorkel and fins and I clutched the heavy little chest in my arms. "I wonder what's inside." I pondered aloud, filled with the excitement of hugging the weighty prize.

"It's a good thing my mother's making me lunch, and I don't have to depend on our spear fishing skills to eat. Otherwise I'd be going hungry. 'Cause I don't think that box would taste very good." We all joined in Oz's laughter.

After walking back to the shack, we rinsed ourselves off with the hose and cleaned our diving gear. I strapped the chest onto my bicycle, gave Oz and Jimbo a thumbs up and took off.

Back home, my mother had made tomato soup and grilled cheese sandwiches. Awesome! I was famished!

"How was the surf Buzz?" My mom asked. She set the plate of food on the table.

"Flat, so we went snorkeling," I replied. "Mom, you won't believe it, we found a treasure chest." She smiled but her facial expression changed to one of amazement when I pulled the mysterious container out of my backpack.

"Well, if there's treasure in that chest, there's not much of it," she commented. "It certainly is an ancient looking box. Have you been able to open it?" Mom studied the object.

After lunch, I waited for Jimbo all afternoon. He rang the doorbell five minutes before four o'clock. I grabbed the rusty chest off of my desk. It left a wet square stain that ruined the varnish on top, but all I could think about was a treasure that might be in the box.

I shouted to my mom from the back door: "We're going to the locksmith."

"Be back before six o'clock, honey, and good luck. I hope its worth a lot of money so I can afford a housekeeper and your Dad can retire," my mom could not resist a joke!

"Okay, Mom," I hollered back as I slammed the door shut. I then turned to my friend, "Ready, Jimbo?"

"Ten-four, I'm ready," he replied with a tinge of anticipation in his voice. We decided to leave our bikes at my house and walk into town. Jimbo was silent almost the entire journey when he suddenly exploded.

"What about my portion? If there's something valuable in there like gold or jewelry, how are we going to split it up?"

At first, I was surprised. I had never even thought about that. "We'll each get an equal share. Each gets a third. Even, Steven." I told him while switching the box from one arm to the other.

The locksmith's shop was located on Main Street between an ice-cream parlor and a movie rental store. As we entered the storefront, a bell jingled announcing our arrival. We were greeted by a silver-haired man wearing denim coveralls and thick black rimmed glasses from behind the counter. He looked at us suspiciously.

"I'll be with you in a moment, boys," he mumbled before getting back to key cutting. After a minute he turned to us and asked, "So, what can I do for you?" His eyes fixated on the box in my arms. Their pupils were magnified three times by the bifocals he wore on his nose. "What do you have here boys? This box looks very old." He cleared his throat and spoke with a hoarse tone.

"Can you open it?" Jimbo burst out.

"Well, let me see," he replied. Then he grabbed an oil can and lubricated the hinges on either side of the chest. He tapped the lock a few times with a small mallet, turned his back to us, and reached into a drawer. The locksmith pulled out a shiny metal ring with keys attached to it. He examined some of the keys on that ring, and dropped it back into the drawer. During the entire time, he whistled to a tune playing on an old-time radio behind the counter. He retrieved another ring with stranger looking keys attached to it.

"Okay, let's see now." The locksmith focused his eyes on the box through the bottom lenses of his bifocal glasses. He tried every single key. Jimbo and I watched him with wordless intensity. The only sound in the room was the clinking of the keys in the locksmith's hands. He tried to open the small chest, but the top would only move slightly so he picked up the mallet again and tapped the hinges then placed it back down on the counter. Again he tried to pull the lid up. Still, it refused to budge.

"This little box has been under water for a while; I can see by the corrosion and the dampness inside the lock." He noticed. "Not to mention, these prickly barnacles are making it tougher to handle." As he spoke, the locksmith's attention never left the object. He picked up a straight edge screwdriver in his left hand and the mallet in his right hand and guided the sharp edge of the screwdriver along the lid of the chest, scraping off pieces of shell, rusted metal, and barnacles. While he tapped the mallet's handle, he banged all the way around the box and back again.

Finally, he took the straight edge of the screwdriver and tapped upwards against the lock in the chest. TAP TAP TAP TAP...CLICK! Our jaws dropped as the lid of the chest popped up! We both rushed around behind the counter to take a look inside.

"Aw, a soggy book!" Jimbo could not hide the disappointment in his voice.

Yes, it looked like some kind of an illegible diary or record book with a warped leather cover. It was nestled snuggly inside the chest, as if it were made for the booklet to fit perfectly within. Jimbo tried to lift the cover from the book. All of the pages were stuck together like a block, and the mushy paper felt like a slimy square sponge. We stared at what was supposed to have been a great discovery.

"Is that all I can assist you with, boys?" The locksmith seemed annoyed that we had joined him behind the counter.

"That will be five dollars," he announced as he put his tools away, after wiping each one with a chamois.

I reached into my pockets and pulled out my last four dollar bills. Jimbo's scowl had been replaced by a blank look. I narrowed my eyes in his direction and glared at him knowing exactly what he was thinking. My friend, in his usual dramatic fashion, forced a wallet from his back pocket. He grimaced as he pulled one dollar bill from it and laid it down next to mine and murmured: "That's all I've got, man." Then he sighed.

The locksmith smiled and replied, "Thank you gentlemen. Please come again."

He put the money in a cash register behind the desk and returned his attention to the job he was working on prior to our arrival. The door jingled as Jimbo walked out. After snatching the box from the counter and exiting the shop, Jimbo was waiting for me on the sidewalk beside a lamp post, kicking stones into the street.

"What a waste! You might as well throw that thing in the garbage!" Jimbo shrugged the whole thing off.

I held onto the box tightly. "I think I'll keep it if you don't mind."

"Sure, I don't care. Go ahead and keep it, you paid for most of the locksmith's bill and you were the one who found the silly box. I'll call Oz and tell him we didn't find a fortune." Jimbo was instantly finished with our adventure.

We left Main Street and headed back towards my house, disappointed. Even though there was no treasure in it, I held onto the box like it was a prize. I was determined to dry the book out. Maybe there was a secret message. Maybe there was a map? Why else would a book be kept under lock and key and hidden in the ocean?

# CHAPTER 7
## A Hidden Etching

The next day I didn't hear the usual morning racket when I woke up. My parents' bedroom door was closed and Eric was still quiet. They were all sleeping late. Mom wasn't making breakfast so I slid down the banister and slipped softly into the kitchen. I reached for a bowl and a box of my favorite cereal from the cupboard. There was still a half gallon of milk in the refrigerator. I finished every last spoonful of the cereal and drank the milk in the bowl before writing a note for my parents: "GONE SURFING WITH OZ & JIMBO, USUAL SPOT, BACK BY NOON—BUZZ"

With my wetsuit in my backpack, I jumped on my bike and headed for the shack. When I arrived at our hideout, I realized I was the first one there. Oz appeared minutes later. He raced all the way up to the gate and slammed on the brakes of his bicycle, leaving a rubber skid mark all the way up the alley.

"Are you ready? Where's Jimbo?" Oz blurted out as he jumped off his bike.

"Look behind you."

Jimbo was pedaling his bike down the alley in a leisurely fashion.

"Slow poke!" Oz snickered.

"Na-ah! I got stuck at the light," Jimbo protested.

We waited for Jimbo and then entered the shack to put

on our wetsuits. Jimbo pulled his gear out of his backpack. A putrid smell filled the room. It was foul!

"Hey guys, did anyone check the surf yet?" Didn't he notice the stench?

"Nope," Oz and I both responded while staring at Jimbo's wetsuit.

"Maybe we shouldn't put our wetsuits on. What if it's flat?" He questioned.

"Something stinks. Who didn't rinse their wetsuit?" I asked.

We both looked at Jimbo, who seemed to have no clue. Oz finally broke the silence and spoke out: "Jimbo, your wetsuit smells like death. You need to rinse it with fresh water and dry it after every use. You always take your suit off after we surf and leave it on the floor. No wonder the shack stinks!"

I couldn't help laughing it up with Oz. "Especially when you urinate in your wetsuit," I teased Jimbo with special emphasis on the word 'urinate.' He shrugged us off and promised to rinse it out in the future.

It was late, 8:45 a.m. The sun had already climbed the sky. Since it was summer, there were already many surfers speckling the water. Four foot waves pounded the shore due to a huge storm that was creating the swell far out to sea. Naturally, the radio was announcing this grand surf-report on every station. When we reached the bottom steps to the beach, the soles of my feet felt the sun's warmth in the soft white sand. Our trio wove its way through the colony of beach towels and umbrellas that decorated the shoreline. We tossed our backpacks under the wooden lifeguard tower, which already had a bunch of T-shirts and towels hanging from its stilted cross-supports.

As we strolled by the front of the tower, we heard a lifeguard shout: "G'day, mates," in a thick Australian accent from the top of the structure. There sat Nate wearing a brim straw hat. His nose was slathered with white creamy zinc oxide. It's used as sun protection for people who spend a lot of time outdoors. Otherwise their skin becomes burned.

"Good-day, mate," Jimbo replied as Oz and I waved at our favorite lifeguard. He smiled at us, but immediately shifted his gaze back to the swarm of people in the water. We waxed the decks of our surfboards, sharing a small clump that I managed to salvage from the pocket of my baggies. The heat of the golden morning sun made the wax sticky on our surfboards as we trekked down to the shoreline.

The ocean was inviting and warm. A school of tiny silvery fish darted in front of us, as we waded through the clear shallow waters. Oz, Jimbo, and I charged out to the ocean in a V-formation as a wave of foam pushed its way past us. While the water grew deeper, we jumped onto our boards and paddled towards the breaking waves. The surge was more forceful the farther out we paddled. A larger set of rollers came in. I noticed a wall of white foam approaching Oz, who was about fifteen feet ahead of our pack. He pushed his surfboard down and ducked his head into the looming breaker. The last thing I saw of him was his left leg pointing toward the sky. Then the wall of white water totally engulfed Jimbo. Out of the corner of my eye, I saw the ocean clobber him. POWWW! The oncoming wave roared loudly before I felt the enormous, SLAMMM, hit me too. My arms were powerless. I hugged my board to no avail, as the wave tore it from my grip before rolling me around like a rag doll. It felt like a tremendous force grabbing my surfboard and ripping it out from below me. I was tossed in an orbit, tumbling underneath the sea until the force passed and the wave released my body from its grip. Finally, after reaching the ocean's surface, I took a deep gulp of air.

"WOW, these waves have some juice!" I screamed to myself yanking the leash to retrieve my surfboard. Jimbo was already further out and diving under the next approaching wave. I quickly slid back onto my surfboard and headed straight towards a roller, remembering that the key to a successful duck dive is timing.

The next tower of water approached. Using all the strength that I could muster, I drove the front section of my surfboard straight down beneath me into the ocean. Once submerged, I pushed the board deeper with my right foot and forced my trunk down onto the surfboard. I was lying flat on the deck, several feet under the water's surface. The breaker rushed over me, and the nose of my surfboard popped out of the other side of the wave, with me tightly gripping the rails.

"Yeah, that's more like it!" I shouted in the roar of the waves. I felt so free. I didn't care if anyone could hear me talking to myself. Paddling out to join the others in the lineup, I could catch glimpses of surfers racing up and down the faces of waves that were slightly higher than their heads. Each approaching wall of water boosted my excitement.

Jimbo and Oz both caught perfect waves. They rode and hooted as I continued to paddle to the take off spot. Oz was the first to launch flying down the face of one of the glassy blue walls. His stance on the surfboard was wide and solid. He looked like a matador confident in the face of a dangerous bull as he raced by the other surfers, locking his eyes in the direction of the shore. Jimbo caught the next wave of the set. He has a very unique and unusual surfing style. When he's riding a wave, he appears to be made out of rubber contorting his body into positions that most people cannot achieve. Crouching forward, Jimbo dropped down the wave's face. Then he carved a bottom turn and with his arms flapping, sliced straight back up the wave.

Within seconds, Jimbo too had passed from my sight. He had caught the final wave of that set, so I knew the ocean would calm itself for a moment. I took that opportunity to paddle swiftly without the resistance of incoming waves. The water surface was still white and foamy from the breakers that had passed. The fine bubbles in the ocean made a fizzing sound around me, as if I was swimming in a can of soda.

All but two of the surfers had caught rides and the rest of the pack was now headed back out from the inside. The duo that had been left behind didn't seem bothered. They were older men sitting on their long boards, locked deep in conversation with each other. Moving past them, a few yards further out, I tried to position myself in the right spot to catch the next wave. I'm fortunate. My long distance vision is excellent. It enables me to see sets of waves approaching from the horizon before most other surfers in the lineup can. That way I always get a paddling head start and can quickly shift into position to seize a ride. There! On the horizon, I saw the next set of breakers coming toward me. I glanced back toward the shore, hoping that the pack of surfers hadn't caught up to my take-off spot in the lineup. I was in luck. The closest surfer was still ten yards away.

As the first wave rose, I spun my surfboard around and paddled with all my might in its direction towards the shore. I could feel the power. After only four arm strokes I felt the swell's tight grip pulling my board. In an instant, I jumped to my feet, free falling down the wave's face. Out of the corner of my eye, I saw the two long boarders still sitting on their sticks admiring my ride. One of them hooted as I accelerated down the wave and pulled a smooth bottom turn towards my right. That maneuver changed my path from speeding straight towards the beach to racing in a direction parallel to the shoreline. I glided ahead of the curl as some of the returning surfers scrambled out of my path over the face of the wave.

Instinctively, I cutback when I felt my surfboard slowing because I had allowed myself to race too far ahead of the wave's curve. I turned my surfboard in the opposite direction and then back one-hundred and eighty degrees to my left, smack in the path of the breaking wave. Within a split second, I was back near the approaching curl, and had to snap another quick 180 degree turn. I slowed for a brief moment. When I was back in the zone on the wave, my surfboard gained enough speed for me to race up and down the wall of water. My arms were outstretched as the thrill of the adrenaline from the ride filled my body. I was flying!

The wave continued to propel me towards the shore. As I rushed nearer to the shallow water just a few yards from the sand, the entire wave crumbled. I fell off my surfboard, totally worn out after the long ride. My body made a clumsy, SPLASH, and THUMP, into six inches of water and onto the sandy ocean bottom. WOW, what a wave! I relished in the sun's warmth while taking a moment to catch my breath in the shallow water. After wiping the salt water out of my eyes and rising to my feet, I waded back into the waist deep sea. Reaching for my surfboard, I squinted in the direction of the lineup as another surfer caught a large wave and began to paddle back for more.

After an hour and an extreme tidal change, the ocean seemed to have suddenly gone flat. We strolled back to the shack, exhausted. On the way we exchanged stories about the great waves we rode and the fantastic maneuvers we had performed. We even shared a laugh or two at some other surfers' blunders. We rinsed out our wetsuits, and Jimbo finished first as usual.

"I wasn't joking. No wonder your wetsuit stinks," Oz teased, then in a serious tone said: "You gotta really rinse thoroughly, Jimbo." Jimbo rolled his eyes at Oz.

That night, before going to sleep, I turned on my lamp and began thumbing through the pages of a comic book. I felt heroic after conquering the day's swell. It was scorching hot and I was still wearing my baggies, too tired to change into my pajamas. Instead, I laid there looking up toward the rotating blades of my ceiling fan, not even remembering the page I just read. My gaze drifted around the room. The chest caught my eye; it was still on my desk where I had left it the day before. The cover of the box was tilted up and the reading lamp cast a beam onto it. I noticed dim scratches on the inside surface of the chest's lid. My eyes focused, and I moved closer to examine the faint lines. The shadow from my body blocked the light and the lines vanished. I rubbed the surface of the chest's cover, but still could not make out the words. I saw this in a movie, I thought to myself. Maybe that trick with the pencil and paper would work here. I cracked my drawer open and pulled out a yellow pencil. It was only two inches long and the eraser top had long been used up, but it would do just fine. I opened the drawer further and pulled out a sheet of binder paper. I ripped the page in half and positioned it on the inside of the chest cover. Bit by bit an impression began to reveal itself as I faintly shaded a section in with my pencil. As I continued, letters began to take shape. Slowly, the words "Turtle Cave" became visible. My heart began to pound as I continued, until a subtle sketch emerged that resembled the crude illustration of a cave. The scratches depicted the head and front flippers of a turtle protruding from above the cavern's entrance.

"Turtle Cave!" I blurted out and tip-toed downstairs to the phone, grabbed the receiver and dialed Jimbo's telephone number. The line was busy so I hung up and dialed Oz's number. It rang.

"Hola," Oz's mother answered with a soft Spanish accent.

"Buenos noches, Senora Gonzales. This is Buzz. Can I please speak with Oz?"

"No sorry, he is already sleeping. Call in the morning."

"Oops, I apologize for calling so late." I glanced at the wall clock. It was already past ten o'clock.

"Your Spanish is improving, though. Buenos noches, Buzz," Oz's mother complimented me before she hung up the telephone.

Suddenly, I heard creaking noises coming from upstairs. "Buzz, are you still up?" My father's annoyed voice boomed down the staircase.

"No, sir, just getting a drink of water," I answered.

"Goodnight, son." His tone softened.

I went back to bed and couldn't relax most of the night. Every few minutes I had to open my eyes and look at the chest and the drawing to make sure it wasn't a dream. When I finally fell asleep, my dreams were full of caves with turtles and hidden treasure. The next morning I woke up real early. I wanted to beat my friends to the shack and share my discovery about the chest and Turtle Cave. I hopped on my bike and pedaled toward the beach.

"Good morning, Buzz," Nana called out from the back window when I arrived. "Let me know if you need anything. I'll bring some peach iced-tea out later."

I glanced over my shoulder and waved. Just then the gate creaked open. "Hi, my mom said you called last night." Oz walked into the yard and waved to Nana, who smiled and returned the greeting from her window.

"You're going to think I'm crazy, but listen to me." I said.

Oz shrugged his shoulders and didn't seem too enthusiastic. He grabbed a rake and began removing the leaves and rotten berries from the lawn which had fallen from the large tree above.

"What's so urgent Buzz, sounds like you won the lottery." He continued raking.

I decided to wait until all three of us were in the shack before sharing my discovery. Reaching for a metal weeding tool, I began digging out the dandelions that crowded the lawn. Finally, after about half an hour later, Jimbo stormed into the yard, behind schedule as usual.

"Sorry I'm late guys," he panted repentantly.

"Buzz has something to tell us." Oz continued raking.

"Follow me into the shack," I dropped my gardening tool. Jimbo and Oz looked at each other, and then followed.

"The secret of the box is in the lid. We were too fast to dismiss it as junk. Look at this." I pulled out the chest and placed it on the floor, then showed my friends the rubbing of the inside of the lid that revealed the faint lines.

"So?" Jimbo looked at me blankly.

Oz was quiet. He examined the chest and grabbed the piece of paper that revealed the sketch of a cave. Oz took the pencil and repeated the experiment again and the same diagram appeared on a piece of paper.

"I think you've got something here." Oz announced wrinkling his brow. "But what does it mean?" His voice puffed.

"I don't know, looks like a map or a clue to a puzzle." I speculated.

"Or it's a cryptogram!" Jimbo added.

"We must figure out what this means." I paused and was almost afraid to tell them that I had dreamt that the sketch was of a cave where buried treasure was hidden. My friends would surely make fun of me. Instead, I murmured: "Maybe there's an actual Turtle Cave around here."

"Hmm," Oz was deep in thought. "You might be absolutely correct. The problem will be figuring out the cave's location, if it is..." He paused for a moment and continued, "...if it is anywhere near here. We could go to the library and research whether any books or magazines have photographs of caves in the area. For all we know, this might be a sketch of a cavern half way around the world." Oz was always a realist.

"I know about some books with historical pictures of our local coast at the public library." Jimbo could not hide his excitement.

"We should go research tomorrow," I suggested.

"Sure," Oz kept staring at the paper.

Jimbo's voice was getting louder. "Last year, I wrote a report for school. My Geography class was assigned a project where we had to demonstrate how the coastline and cliffs in the area have changed over time. I copied pictures of the shoreline from the old books and compared them with recent photographs of the same locations as they appear today. Some sites were the same, and others were changed by erosion." Jimbo could not contain himself anymore. "Why wait 'til tomorrow! We can go to the library after lunch."

"I have a couple of books I need to return anyway." I piped in. "Let's not tell anyone about this." I added.

They nodded in agreement. Jimbo managed the noisy grass cutter while Oz and I continued raking leaves and shaping bushes in front of Nana's house. Nearly two hours later, we were washing our hands with the garden hose admiring our landscaping job. It almost appeared as if a professional had groomed it.

"My, this looks wonderful." Nana stepped out of the backdoor holding a tray with a pyramid of sandwiches and a pitcher of iced tea on it.

"Right on, food!" Jimbo's eyes widened at the sight of the tasty grub.

"Thank you," Oz grabbed a sandwich nearly knocking the tray over.

"Manners, get some." Jimbo gave Oz a dirty look.

"Thanks Nana," I said delicately taking a sandwich.

Nana sounded like she was yodeling announcing, "There's more where this came from. You boys did such a good job and worked so hard, you must be starving. Oh, the landscaping looks wonderful!"

None of us could respond because our mouths were stuffed with the delicious lunch Nana had made. Our thoughts were on Turtle Cave.

# CHAPTER 8
## The Library

We met at three o'clock, at the Beach Branch of the public library. My mom had some borrowed books to return too, so she drove me there and naturally brought little Eric along. Jimbo and Oz had already arrived and were in the reading room with a towering stack of books in front of them. Jimbo was sitting in a chair while Oz stood to his left leaning on the table. They were both eyeing a tattered old book as Jimbo turned the pages. I approached my friends. My mom walked toward the fiction section with my little brother in tow. He watched us longingly as she dragged him away. We had business to take care of, and this was no time for little brothers!

"Find anything yet?" I asked my friends.

"Nope," Jimbo answered while skimming through the first book.

"We just started." Oz whispered to me as he put his index finger over his lips. "We don't want anybody to hear our secret."

I pulled out the empty chair to Jimbo's right and sat down. Oz finally sat Indian-style on the large wooden library table. We huddled over an old book. The cover was made out of dark leather adorned with gold calligraphy, and it was full of black and white photographs of the coastline. We went through it page by page. There was not even a reference to a 'Turtle Cave.'

Some pictures showed cliffs and rock formations, and others depicted the towns in our area the way they appeared many, many years ago. Other photographs showed beaches lined with caverns, but there was no mention of a Turtle Cave anywhere in that volume. Jimbo closed the first book, shoved it over to me, and retrieved a second from the pile next to Oz. There were some interesting pictures in that edition too, but still nothing even came close to resembling the clue we required to explain our mystery.

Mom took Eric home. She knew better than to let Eric around us. We were 'The Grommets' now and little brothers were not included. Not one of the books we thumbed through revealed an answer to the mystery of Turtle Cave. We searched each publication page by page, and when we finally reached the last book, we had still found nothing!

"Maybe we should thumb through each volume again. Let's check these books out and take them home. We can divide this batch between us and search each book more carefully," I suggested.

Oz nodded in agreement.

"Yeah, I guess," Jimbo sighed, as he took off his steel rimmed glasses and rubbed his eyes. "Besides, I hate the library; it's too quiet in here."

We dealt the heap into three piles, and each of us chose a stack.

"Do you want to check the surf on the way home, guys?" I asked glancing at my friends.

"Sure," Oz perked up as he rose to his feet, and pushed the chair back under the library table. He sounded eager to get out of there.

"Nah, I've got to head home." Jimbo responded wearily. His newly found enthusiasm for the mystery was beginning to weaken.

We followed Jimbo to the bicycle rack. He unlocked his cruiser and strapped the books with his chain lock on the back frame to secure them. "Okay, see you investigators later." He flashed us a military salute while swinging a leg over his bicycle seat for the race home.

"Call me if there's any surf. We'll go out tomorrow." Those were Jimbo's last words as he bounced his front wheel off the curb and bolted across the street. With his backpack loaded with books and more strapped to the luggage rack on his bike, he pedaled at break-neck speed pausing only to round the corner. Oz and I headed home with our piles of books.

After a few minutes of silence, I questioned my friend. "Do you think we'll ever find Turtle Cave or a treasure?"

"It's fun trying to crack a mystery, kind of like working to solve a puzzle." Oz smiled as he shifted his stack of books from one arm to the other and added, "I sure wouldn't complain if we did find a treasure, though. The first thing I'd do is go down to the surf shop and buy ten new boards."

We laughed and shared ideas about what we would do if we struck gold.

# CHAPTER 9
## Turtle Cave

We did not discover anything in the books we brought home from the library. The next week, Jimbo left town for his yearly summer visit with his grandparents. Oz and I arranged to meet at the shack for a surf session. I arrived early, or so I thought, and parked my bicycle at the gate. I toted my surfboard, wetsuit and towel out of the shack and dropped them on the lawn which was overgrown and wild. Then I saw something curious. I noticed Oz's surfboard lying on the floor in the shack with his backpack on top of it. 'Hmm,' I wondered to myself. 'Where is Oz?' Just then, in the background, I could hear the slapping of his feet on the pavement as he scurried up the alley to the shack.

"Hey!" Oz was breathless.

"Howzit?" I greeted him.

"I got here an hour ago." Oz was still panting for air as he continued to speak. "I went to the cliffs and discovered a clean little wave with nobody out. Let's hurry before the tide and wind change and turn the ocean back to a lake." Oz ranted excitedly.

"No way, the cliffs are not an area I'm allowed to surf at." I blurted.

"It's okay, we'll be safe together. Let's surf!" Oz grabbed his board and backpack. I paused for a second, then threw my wetsuit and towel over my shoulder, grabbed the handlebar with one hand and jumped on my bike.

Already on his way to the forbidden surf area, Oz turned the corner and vanished from my sight. I had to pedal faster and increase my pace to catch up because Oz was already on the next block. He peered over his shoulder and slowed his speed until I caught up with him. After about five blocks, Oz directed his bicycle right towards the ocean through a neighborhood with older majestic homes. Colossal mature trees lined both sides of the wide avenue. Since there were no cars on the road, I pulled up next to Oz and we rode side by side. At the end of the street, the trees cleared. We were nearing the ocean cliff zone. Oz crossed a street and turned onto a narrow dirt path. The earth on the pathway was packed hard and smooth, and was easy to ride our bikes on. We peddled for a few more minutes until the road led us to the edge of a cliff. Oz smiled gazing at the ocean about a hundred feet below. He glanced at the tidal watch Nana gave him. I checked mine, too.

"The conditions are similar to before when I checked nearly an hour ago. The waves should even improve with the outgoing tide." Oz's eyes were fixed on the ocean as he spoke confidently.

"Wow," was all that I could utter as I watched a set of three-foot waves below us peeling with near perfection. "But... how do we get down there?" Reality hit me. We had to descend the cliff somehow, and it was a long drop below.

"Don't worry. There's a trail over there." Oz replied as he pointed north.

Somehow my friend's confidence didn't ease my anxiety, but the waves looked really fun and the surf wasn't breaking anywhere else. For a split second, I thought of revealing my fears to Oz. The cliff appeared too steep and scary for me to handle. But when another glassy emerald three-foot wave peeled below us, and then two more chased behind, I decided to keep my thoughts quiet.

"Okay, I'll follow you," I informed Oz.

"Hooray for your bravery," Oz encouraged.

He dropped his left leg over the seat of his bicycle as it fell to the ground and embarked down a very narrow footpath, which led to a steep vertical drop for about ten feet until the trail leveled out below. Oz slipped halfway down the sharp section of the path, but regained his balance and jogged downhill the rest of the way. I also made the sudden drop about halfway down before my feet began to slip under me in the sand.

"Yaow!" I yelped.

Like a skier with both feet parallel, holding on to my surfboard overhead, I glided over the remainder of the sandy path, relieved that I didn't fall flat on my face. Oz was waiting several feet from where I finally stopped descending. He greeted me with his intense white smile. We had made it down the steepest cliff. As we marched onward, I was captivated by the unfamiliar landscape. We traversed a little sand canyon with steep high cliff walls surrounding us. Except for the section of earth we had slid down, the walls were too vertical to climb or hike.

"Let's put our wetsuits on here." Oz directed as he carefully placed his surfboard on the dirt and pulled his short sleeved spring suit out of his backpack.

After stepping into the legs of his wetsuit and pulling it up over his surf trunks, he stuffed his T-shirt into the backpack and grabbed his board. The sun was hot and I was sweating. The rubber material from my suit was sticking to my skin. A welcome cooling sea breeze blew up from the shore. We strolled further down the path to the ravine, which led to a shelf. Oz walked along the cliff's edge until he encountered a location where we could easily descend. He dropped his backpack down to the rocky beach. It made a THUD, sound below. I watched as Oz placed his surfboard down a few feet back from the ledge.

The shoreline was made up of gray boulders of varying sizes. Skipping from rock to rock is tricky. You have to choose your own path. Most of the rocks were stable, but some of the smaller ones wobbled when our feet made contact. Others were very slippery due to splashing sea water and algae growth, and were difficult to traverse while trying to balance ourselves carrying our surfboards. The wall of the cliff cut off at the beach's end creating a barrier. After hiding our backpacks behind a car size boulder, we navigated our way down to a small sandy patch at the shore on the base of the bluff. It was a perfect place to strap our leashes to our ankles and wade into the water towards the surf. Paddling north, we maneuvered around a few smaller rocks which protruded out of the ocean. The sea deepened and the boulders began to vanish while we increased our speed. As usual, Oz was paddling about fifteen feet ahead of me. After reaching deeper water, he sat up on his surfboard and waited for me to catch up to him. My arms were beginning to burn a little from the long paddle.

"Wow, it's a longer journey than I thought it would be," Oz confessed. "But once we clear that rock, we'll be able to see the waves breaking." He insisted reassuringly. He pointed to a massive boulder jutting out from the base of the cliff at the shoreline.

Oz started paddling again, and I chased behind. Three huge, white seagulls with red spots on their beaks parked themselves on the boulder. They watched us curiously as we passed by. After we finally maneuvered around another enormous rock, a long stretch of the coastline became visible.

Now the reef and the waves were within our sight. Each time a breaker rushed through and broke ahead of us, we hooted for joy and then paddled even faster. I completely forgot the burning in my arms when spinning my surfboard around to catch my first wave. With two more commanding arm strokes, I immediately felt the pull on my board and a welcome rush of water on my back. Adrenaline pulsed through my body and I jumped to my feet. Instantly, I veered right for a brief flash before shooting up to the wave's crest, then plummeting back down. Several more off-the-lip turns enabled me to increase my speed and race through the next section of the shimmering wall as I glided up and over the top. For a short moment, I was riding in back of the wave. With a quick sharp turn, I reentered its face! After a few more yards of elated flight, the wave collapsed, crumbling into mushy white bubbles. I kicked out, swiveled my surfboard around, and dropped down to lay flat on the deck. I was eager to paddle back out towards the take-off spot.

We were all alone. In the distance, I could see Oz catching his next wave. He paddled, jumped up, dropped, and turned left. Immediately, he jammed his left arm into the face of the breaker, which slightly slowed his speed. As his momentum decreased, the curl of the toppling wave caught up with him. Oz disappeared in its tube as the lip pitched out over him. A split second later, his head popped up on the ocean's surface next to his surfboard. I could hear him laughing. The first roller of the next set passed. It was not powerful enough to peak, so I waited for another. I paddled and caught a ride with minor effort and only a few arm strokes. I sprung to my feet and plummeted straight down the beautiful breaker. This time I had more speed, sending my surfboard racing past a steep section of sea as the ocean rose behind me. I arched up the wave's wall and banked an off the lip turn as I was carried back down the line. My speed slowed, so I did a cutback. The peak was about shoulder high, and I whipped a turn back in the other direction just in time. My surfboard stalled for a fraction of a second, until I sensed the surge pushing me through the wall's next section. Finally, the breaker exhausted itself and slowed me to a snail's pace. I crouched down and rode the white water.

"The lefts are fun!" Oz roared, as he paddled towards me. "And there's a cave over there at the shore. I think you need to take a look at it!" Oz screamed while pointing with exhilaration as I rode by him.

Normally, I would have kicked out of the ride sooner, but after being intrigued by what Oz had said, I dropped down onto my surfboard for a closer look. I reached forward and grabbed the nose and rode the rest of the wave lying on my belly towards the shoreline. Pushing down on the nose of my surfboard I tried to get every last bit of forward momentum. It wasn't safe surfing close to rocks and cliffs, but I wanted to see the cave. The clear water revealed a crimson and jade sea bottom carpeted with ocean plants and sea life. The wave dropped me off in a pocket of calm water. A variety of sea anemones blanketed the rocky underwater ridge; meanwhile a school of small fish caught my attention as they darted underneath me. Paddling nearer to the cliff, there was a large section of rock that protruded out from the main overhang like a giant block. It was about thirty feet wide.

I moved in closer wondering what was behind the massive stone. It appeared as if the huge section of the cliff had broken off and was pushed out to sea. I turned around the corner and glided into an area of glassy calm water with steep walls surrounding me. Glancing up, I was startled by what was in front of me and shouted: "IT'S THE TURLE CAVE!" The cavern was concealed and sheltered behind the detached cliff. It was truly amazing! Sitting up on my board with my back arched and my eyes locked toward the sky, the cavern appeared vast. Most importantly, above the cave's entrance revealed a natural sculpture of the front side of a sea turtle! A huge boulder shaped like a turtle's head protruded from the summit of the cavern's opening, while two oblong stones resembling tortoise flippers rested at the sides of its head. Many smaller boulders clumped together at the pinnacle mimicked a turtle's upper shell. I sat up on my surfboard in the serene water. After rubbing my eyes in disbelief, I opened them again and stared up. I wasn't dreaming. The cavern and the turtle shaped formation were still there! Sitting there dumbfounded, I just could not believe it, staring at the sculpture's eye slits and the turtle's wide grin. Then I paddled closer to the entrance of the cavern.

Over my shoulder, I saw Oz approaching me.

"Do you see what I mean?" He shouted.

"Yeah, this is exactly what we were looking for." I raved. "Wow!"

Oz paddled next to me sitting up on his knees. "Let's explore the cave." He went ahead and a tidal surge pulled us into the cave's foyer. The entrance was black and it took a few minutes for my eyes to adjust to the low dim light. The air and water remained tranquil except for our splashing. There was a musty odor. We drifted deeper where the cavern's ceiling was at least twenty feet high. My friend and I left our boards floating and waded over to the rocks inside its isolated interior. We climbed out of the sea onto some sharp stones, and noticed a solid rock floor past the rocks. I peered over my shoulder and realized the only illumination in the cave remained near its entrance from the shining sun outside far away. Our feet pattered in unison as the water trickled down from our wetsuits and left salty puddles on the cold earth.

"AYYY-OOO," I shouted as the roar of my voice echoed throughout the cave.

"OWWW," Oz's voice bounced around the cave walls.

The back of the cavern had a pile of seaweed that was washed in by the tidal surge. It looked like a haystack and was about two feet taller than me. Oz began yanking the seaweed away. I followed his example and grabbed handfuls of the cold slimy kelp. The putrid smell nearly knocked me out.

"Eww!" I blurted. "It stinks in here, smells like rotten eggs!"

The decaying seaweed on the bottom of the pile produced a dreadful odor of sulfur.

"What if we find some treasure under here?" I joked, as we grabbed clumps of the smelly stuff and threw it aside. Removing the kelp revealed an accumulation of bowling ball-sized rocks that were stacked underneath.

"Do you think there's anything under these stones?" I asked Oz. Bits of seaweed and wet sand grains were stuck to his jet black hair and brown skin. My eyes had finally adjusted to the dim light.

"Treasure would be cool," Oz replied, and warned. "Just make sure you don't drop one of these rocks on your foot. You'll break bones."

We took turns lifting the heavy stones, one at a time, and cautiously rolled them down the outside of the stack. After twenty minutes of gradual progress, my body was burning up in my wetsuit even though the cave was chilly. We kept on working. Finally, we made what seemed to be a worthwhile discovery.

"A DOOR!?" We exclaimed in synchronicity with a question of doubt. Yes, it was a thick, hefty wooden door and we had uncovered only the top few inches.

"That's timber alright," Oz declared after scratching the surface with his fingernail.

"Wonder where it leads?" I glanced at my watch. "The tide is changing. It's getting late," I realized aloud. "We could get stuck here at high tide!"

"We'll have to come back and clear the rest another time." Oz replied and pressed the glow button on his watch as he nodded in agreement.

We climbed up the heap of rocks and out of the crater we had formed surrounding the solid wooden barrier.

"I have to figure out how to get that thing open, later." Oz insisted.

We both carefully scrambled down to the water. The boulders wobbled beneath our feet. The sound of our splashes echoed throughout the cave as we leaped into the ocean and swam to our surfboards. They had drifted away and were bobbing next to each other near the cave entrance. We retrieved them and fastened our leashes to our ankles. Paddling outside of the cavern, I was momentarily blinded by the sun's glow. My eyes weren't accustomed to the brilliant daylight. I stared back up at the stone turtle to make sure I wasn't dreaming. We traveled towards the lineup as another set of waves broke on the outside reef.

"Hmm, I think we have time for a few more waves." Oz smiled.

"Yep, just a couple to wash off that smelly, rotten seaweed." I giggled.

We laughed and paddled out to the zone. Following a few

more fun little rides, we headed home, exhausted and overjoyed by the day's events.

# CHAPTER 10
## A Wooden Door

The next morning Oz and I met at the shack early.

"Hey there, Oz, this yard looks pretty good," I admired.

"Yeah, I'm almost finished. Nana went to the market. She told me she'd bake us cookies later. These tools are too heavy for me to carry all of them to the bluff in my backpack. Help me haul these." Oz handed me a flashlight, crowbar, and a chisel. "I borrowed them from my Pop's tool chest. I must return them before he gets home from work."

"No problem." I stuffed the rest of the tools into my backpack on top of my wetsuit.

"Looks like we're going to have to bring our boards and paddle with the tools in our backpacks." Oz suggested. The plan sounded fine to me.

Just as we had done the day before, we rode back to the cliffs through the old neighborhood. I heard and felt the muffled CLANG of the metal tools in my backpack as we sped over the bumpy pavement. Their heaviness rubbed against my shoulders and made the journey tricky with my surfboard under one arm. We parked our bikes in the same spot and locked them together. This time Oz retrieved a pile of leafy branches. He carefully layered one limb on top of the other until our bikes were barely visible.

"There...camouflage," Oz stepped back and admired his achievement proudly.

"Yeah, that's a smart idea. I can hardly even see them now." I was impressed.

We put on our wetsuits at the shoreline and then jumped into the ocean. Paddling my surfboard with a backpack full of heavy tools felt strange. My board sunk several more inches below the sea with the extra weight. There were no waves breaking on the reef that day, so we headed straight to the cavern. The stone turtle greeted us at the cave's entrance. We paddled into the cool darkness of its belly. Instead of letting our surfboards float loose in the cave, we climbed a dry flat rock and pulled them out of the water. Then, we removed our backpacks. Oz reached into his and pulled out a flashlight.

"It's waterproof!" He proclaimed proudly as he switched it on and aimed the beam into the direction of the mysterious wooden door.

We carried the tools and climbed into the boulder crater. The door was there just as we had left it. Oz handed me the flashlight and I turned it on. The barrier was made of vertical rough cut boards of wood, fastened next to each other with rusty iron nails. Two metal bars were cemented horizontally to the cave wall holding the hatch in place. At first, Oz tried to pry one of the rods off with the crowbar I had hauled from the shack. It didn't work at all. Each time he stuck an end of the tool behind one of the metal bars, it would not budge. Beads of sweat began to drip from his forehead.

"This isn't working," Oz muttered after his final useless attempt.

"Let me try," I said handing the flashlight over to him. I grabbed a hatchet and began chopping at the center of the solid door.

THUMP, THUMP, THUMP, sounded the chopping of the saturated wood. Small chips of damp lumber flew through the air as I pounded away. Progress was very slow and minimal. It occurred to me that my parents would have a fit if they had seen me swinging the sharp hatchet in the dim light with no shoes on.

"Be careful," Oz warned. He must have been reading my thoughts. I switched hands because my right arm began to ache, continuing to hammer away at the oak barrier with my left.

"I'm making some progress," I asserted and asked, "You want to try?"

"Okay," Oz handed me the flashlight and reached for an axe from his backpack. "This might work better."

Again, the THUMP, THUMP, THUMP sound of the axe striking the solid wet planks echoed through the cave. We took turns trying tools, and after about a half an hour, were finally able to knock a five-inch diameter hole into the three inch thick door. The wood was damp and dark from being soaked by seawater for so long.

"Now we need a saw," Oz insisted after chipping the edge of the gap we had created in the frame. He dropped the axe and picked up the hacksaw but it would not fit. There was nothing more that we could do with the tools in our possession.

"We'll need to come back with a different saw," Oz shined the flashlight through the aperture in the door and peeked through.

I peered deeper into the hole we had made in the door. There was a continuation of the cavern on the other side.

"We need a better saw," Oz repeated.

"Let's go back and get one," I replied, enthusiastic about the possibility of breaking through the secret entrance and exploring the cave beyond.

We packed up our tools and jumped back on our surfboards. The tide was flowing in, and the water level in the cave was slightly higher. I stared up at the turtle's head as we paddled out of the opening. Oz was peering up too.

"See you soon, we'll be right back!" He shouted up toward the sky saying goodbye to the stone turtle protruding out from the top of the cave entrance.

Paddling back to the shoreline, we decided that only one of us would need to ride to the shack to borrow Nana's wood-saw. The other would stay down on the rocky beach and keep an eye on our gear and tools. We threw flat stones onto the ocean surface to decide who'd journey back to our clubhouse. My rock skipped the most times and traveled the farthest distance, so I got to choose. I decided to stay, so Oz had to ride back. My job was to guard our equipment and relax on the beach.

"It will definitely take at least forty-five minutes," Oz said after he filled his backpack with the tools we didn't need anymore. I was left with the crowbar, hammer, flashlight, and the hatchet.

Oz walked over to the ledge, climbed up like a bug, and quickly disappeared from sight. I spent my time exploring the rocks and gazing at the sea-life in and around the shoreline and tide pools. There were small fish and sea anemones and a variety of other coastal life to survey. I skipped rocks for a while and watched a flock of pelicans dive into the water. Time flew by and before I had a chance to get bored, Oz returned with the narrow flat blade of the saw sticking out of the opening of his backpack.

"That was quick," I said.

"I brought you something." He smiled. "Nana baked a batch of oatmeal cookies. She packed some up for us." He unzipped his backpack and pulled out a brown paper bag filled with a half-dozen warm oatmeal cookies. They smelled heavenly. I reached in and grabbed a lumpy soft cookie. Oz did the same. We sat below the bluffs and munched away.

"If Jimbo were here, he'd finish the entire bag," I joked as I crumpled the bag shut and saved the remainder in my backpack for later.

We grabbed our boards and headed back to the cave. The water felt chillier than it was in the morning and the tide was much higher now. Because of the incoming tide, the secluded sandy beach cove was nearly submerged. The trip seemed to go by even faster as we paddled back to the cavern for the second time that day. We were greeted by the turtle's stone grin. It was closer to the ocean's plane, which had risen with the incoming tide. Once inside the cave, we discovered the water level had risen up to the base of the boulders in front of the door. For the third time in two days, we scrambled up out of the sea, leaving our surfboards floating in the cave. Oz pulled the saw out of his soaking wet backpack and tapped the blade. I removed a flashlight from mine and turned it on, pointing the beam at the wooden obstacle. Our fingers were pruned from being in the water too long. My friend began to slice away. The sound of the tool ricocheted in the cave as the saw shaved slowly through the thick timbre. A few times the blade became stuck and Oz had to pull it back out and start again.

"Okay, it's your turn." Oz looked at me staring into the beam of the flashlight.

Sawing was tough at first, and the sharp edge kept getting jammed because I wasn't holding it straight. After some practice, I got the hang of it. My right arm started to burn and I switched the saw to my left hand. We lost track of the time but were reminded of it, when seemingly out of nowhere, BOOM! An explosion of water hit the outer cave wall. A wave roared into the cavern and splashed over the boulder pile, nearly knocking me off my feet. We were caught off guard and quickly scrambled to grab the saw and flashlight we had dropped.

"Let's get out of here!" I shouted.

My heart was pounding with terror. The blowout of the first wave crashing was enough warning for me. I didn't want to be in the cave when the next one hit! We rapidly grabbed our soaked backpacks. I stuffed the flashlight in mine and swung it over my shoulders as fast as I could. Luckily we had only taken the flashlight and the saw out of our bags, or Oz surely would have lost some of his dad's tools.

"Lookout, here comes another one!" Oz yelled out.

"Oh no, our boards are history!" I screamed holding onto my backpack with one hand, and bracing myself against the far cave wall for the incoming breaker. All I could do was stare with despair at our surfboards, which were about to get whacked. Damage was certain. My heart sunk as I watched my surfboard be tossed around by the narrow wave of white water, and then it smacked directly into Oz's board.

"OUCH!" I cringed, looking at my injured surfboard.

We stood behind the wall of rocks awaiting the next onslaught of waves. Within seconds another wave rammed our boards straight into the pile of boulders that sheltered us. The salty-sea splashed up onto my face, stinging my sunburned cheeks. I could see Oz bracing himself against the rocks out of the corner of my eye. The roar of water echoed with each crashing wave. Another breaker hit the cave, but it was much weaker and didn't splash over the boulders. That was our cue.

"Okay," I shouted. "We survived that set. Let's get out of here!"

Oz scrambled over the rocks and I followed. I swam to my board. By some miracle, it appeared undamaged. What a relief, no dings! We paddled out quickly and made it under the edge of the turtle's grin before the next wave hit. By the time we reached the beach where we had started, my entire body ached with exhaustion. Oz gave me a high five, and I was relieved to be back on solid ground.

"Whew, we made it!" He proclaimed with his feet planted firmly in the sand.

"Where did those waves come from?" I wondered out loud.

"We'd better check the tides more carefully next time. It's easy enough with our new watches." Oz laughed as we trekked back to the bluff.

"If those waves had been any bigger, the boulders would have hit us like cannon balls!" I exclaimed, realizing how close we had been to getting seriously hurt. It felt good to know that we were making progress on this fantastic adventure. Getting through the wooden door was only a matter of time, now.

Oz waited at the top of the cliff as I negotiated the steep grainy path. When he was a few feet away he exclaimed: "You know, this is so unbelievable that I don't even want to tell anyone. I mean it's crazy. Who is going to believe this?" Oz questioned as he tore away the camouflage branches from our bicycles, unlocked them, and hopped on his dirt bike.

When we finally returned to the shack, Oz ripped off his spring suit and somehow still had enough energy to rinse it out. I didn't even bother changing into my clothes and rode home in my wetsuit. The sun was beginning to set, and darkness sluggishly followed. The mild summer air gradually cooled. Cruising home, all that I could think about was the mysterious wooden door. What secrets could be hidden inside that cave?

# CHAPTER 11
## Ding Repair

The next morning, I woke up to sore muscles in my arms from paddling to and from the cavern. I had blisters on my hands from hacking at the wooden door, but barely noticed them because of the excitement over the mystery of Turtle Cave. At breakfast my mind was consumed with questions and thoughts about what lay behind the wooden barrier we had found inside the secret cavern. What's hidden behind that hatch? I wondered, over and over again

"We're going shopping, today. I need you to help me." My mom informed me as I slurped the last gulp of cold milk from my bowl. My heart sank.

"Brush your teeth and get ready. We're going to the mall." Mom's words hit me like a wall of bricks, with a lightning bolt to boot. Instead of exploring the cave and solving a crucial puzzle, I was being dragged to the mall? How was I going to get out of this? I hated going to the mall and looking for bargains because it always meant countless hours of boredom. Shopping does not excite me, unless I'm buying a surfboard, books or music. I know many kids my age think the mall is cool, but I don't. Once you hit a skate park or the beach, there's no comparison. To me, the mall meant trying on clothes, which I despised or listening to my mom's lectures: "You have a bad attitude about shopping, young man," or "aren't you just so precious in that outfit! Yaddah-yaddah, blah blah blah."

I can't wait until I'm a grown-up and can shop where I desire. Surf shops rule. I buy most of my clothes and gear there anyways. I'm friendly with the sales people that work at the local surf shop, and oftentimes see them shredding waves at Main Beach. I tried to call Oz to tell him I couldn't explore the cave, but his phone was busy. Mom announced that Eric was already in the car seat. Great, I thought, what could I do now? It was time to go. After a twenty-minute drive, the car rounded off of the freeway exit toward the colossal square buildings of the mall. Mom parked the car, unloaded the stroller, strapped Eric in, and we were off. First, we had to take a "quick look" at clothes. It never turned out to be quick, in my opinion.

"Keep an eye on your brother," my mom sternly commanded as she entered a fancy clothing store for women.

Sitting down on a bench with Eric already bored out of my mind, I hoped he wouldn't break out into a screaming fit. There wasn't even a chance of slipping away to a payphone to reach Oz. The real torment began when I had to try on clothes. My mother made me parade around the dressing room with new pants. She also made me model shirts, and sweaters, in front of her. She would gaze at me with a look of deep concentration and then say "yes" or "no" or "that's so cute." The latter really bugged me, but I wasn't daring or stupid enough to snap back with smart remarks when I was so defenseless. All I could think about was getting back to the cliffs to explore the cave. My stomach growled. It was nearly lunchtime. We proceeded to a crowded restaurant. I ordered a cheeseburger with french fries and a thick chocolate milk shake, but my mind was on that cave. We then headed to more boring stores for an afternoon of draining torture. Eric fell asleep in his stroller. I hauled the shopping bags and couldn't wait to get home.

As our car pulled into the driveway, my mom told me to be back from the beach before dark. Was she reading my mind? Finally, after an afternoon of agony, I gathered my gear and raced to my bike. The wind cooled my face as I pedaled towards the shack. Nana was in the yard with Poncho when I rode up. The old Rottweiler approached me with dawdling steps while his tail wagged excitedly. He licked my free hand while enjoying being scratched behind his ear.

"Hello, Buzz," Nana greeted me with a jolly grin. "How are you?" She asked me.

"Hi Nana, I'm okay."

"How's your family?" She asked with a genuine concern.

"Very well, I spent the whole day at the mall shopping," I groaned, relieved to be back at the shack.

"Your friend Oz left a few hours ago. He rode away with his surfboard under one arm with a hand-saw sticking out of his backpack. It looked rather suspicious." Nana took a labored step up to the backdoor of her house and mumbled: "Hmmm, I wonder what you boys are up to. If I didn't know you better I'd think you were up to no good."

I didn't respond. There wasn't time to paddle to the cave before dinner, so I left my surfboard at the shack, jumped on my bike and rode towards the historic neighborhood. The sun filtered through the clouds that began rolling in from the sea. Making the last turn before the cliffs, Oz emerged out of the thick evening marine layer and into view.

"Howzit?" I shouted when he was in hearing range.

"Hey," Oz replied out of breath as he raced toward me. "I got the wooden door cleared enough for us to fit through."

"Great!" I hid my disappointment that Oz had gotten into the cave without me.

"I couldn't see anything. My flashlight batteries ran out. It got really dark, like at night with no moon or street lights." Oz reported. "We must go back tomorrow."

"My thoughts exactly," I responded.

We pedaled back to the shack. Oz told me how he struggled for hours and finally removed a big section of the door blocking the passage into the cave. As we glided through the evening mist, he heard about my awful experience at the mall. We arrived at the shack and leaned our bikes against the fence outside.

Oz headed straight for the hose and rinsed off his face and wetsuit. He pulled the saw out of his backpack and then a large chunk of wood from the saturated door. I could tell that it came from the timber barrier inside Turtle Cave.

"Look here. I brought back a souvenir for the shack," Oz joked as he tossed the dark piece of wood at me.

"Cool," I said admiring the damp heavy block.

"We can have it examined and carbon dated for age if we want. Maybe we can even make a sign out of it, and hang it on the front of our clubhouse. We can carve "The Grommets" in it," I suggested. "I asked my dad what a "Grommet" is, and he told me it's what older surfers call a dedicated, young soul surfer. I guess you could say Grommets are surfer kids, not airplane parts."

"The sign sounds like a neat idea, Buzz. I'd say according to your dad's definition we sure are Grommets!" Oz laughed.

"Anyway, it's late, and my mom will kill me if I'm not home on time. Can you clean up around here?" I shot Oz a pleading look.

"No problem, at least we can check out the entrance to the passage tomorrow." Oz suggested while turning off the sprinkler. "I hope we get waves soon," he added.

"Yeah, I don't think I'll get dragged to the mall two days in a row," I replied and left.

The next morning I called Oz and we met at the shack early. We both brought stronger flashlights and extra batteries. After organizing the tools Oz had borrowed from his dad, we began our expedition. The bike ride journey and trek down to the rocky beach were now becoming routine. Oz carried his backpack into the water. My flashlight was safely stored in an airtight plastic bag with a zipper, which I tucked under my chest while I paddled my surfboard. The surf was still very flat and the ocean was calm and glassy. We arrived at the cave in no time, and I lightheartedly greeted the stone turtle sculpture.

"We're back!" I shouted to the rocky image above me steering into the cave.

We cackled as our voices interrupted the cave's tranquility. The tide was low and there were plenty of rocks above the water level to shelter our surfboards from danger. I couldn't help peering over my shoulder, towards the entrance. Our last experience with the breakers blasting through the cavern left me much more cautious.

"I'm sure the waves that hit the cave last time must have been from the wake of a big ship out to sea," Oz spoke authoritatively.

"You may be right, but we better be careful in the future. It could happen again at anytime." I declared.

"One of us should always keep an eye on the ocean." Oz added after thinking for a moment. "I wish Jimbo were here with us, he'd make a great lookout man."

We turned on our flashlights and scrambled over the rocks. Some of the seaweed we had removed had been washed back against the door. It was a slippery incline. At the top of the pile of boulders, I shined my flashlight against the barrier. The artificial beam exposed a two-foot diameter hole in the wood planks.

"Good job, Oz!" I was stoked to see the large gap in the wooden barrier he had hacked out for us to crawl through.

"I guess we're not waiting for Jimbo after all," I asserted with bravery. Eager to see what was on the other side, I wasted no time entering the passage which was about five feet high. It felt a little spooky. The air was cold and musty. Pausing to make sure Oz was right behind me, I whispered: "Wow, we don't want to get trapped in here," as my heart pounded. Oz extracted a piece of chalk out of his backpack, and etched an 'X' on the cave wall.

"There, 'X' marks the spot," He announced. Oz immediately continued to draw an arrow on the wall pointing in the direction we were exploring. The passage went on about fifty yards. Then it became pitch black. No sunlight reached this far inside the cave. The glow of our flashlights didn't help much to ease my discomfort.

"Do you think we should turn back?" I asked.

"Let's walk a bit further" Oz countered.

He drew another chalk arrow on the wall, and then passed me intensely peering forward. We marched further. I glanced back and the light from the entrance was just a dim slit in the distance.

Oz halted and exclaimed: "This passage is endless! I don't think we are prepared. We need to bring better flashlights and other stuff. Maybe we should turn back and wait to explore with Jimbo."

To my relief, we changed direction and made our way back to the entrance.

"We'll wait for Jimbo next time," Oz agreed.

"We definitely need shoes, helmets, stronger flashlights and extra batteries. It would not be fun to get lost down here." He concluded.

Our surfboards and equipment were exactly where we had left them. The paddle from Turtle Cave back to the shore passed quickly. I was able to propel my surfboard faster than ever before! We returned to the shack, unloaded our gear, and spent the rest of the morning riding retro skateboards we found up in the rafters of our newly inherited clubhouse. Nana said her son used to love the sport when he was our age. The alleys in her neighborhood have a variety of banks and curves which provide amusing skateboarding terrain. Sometimes I'd imagine that I was carving turns through endless waves. Except for falling on the pavement is usually much more painful than smacking against the ocean's surface in small waves. Once you hit a pebble or a shard of glass, reality kicks in as you feel your body striking the cement. Falling off of a skateboard usually involves pain or injury, at least for me. That's why it's always necessary for anyone to wear safety gear and a helmet when you ride cement.

Oz and I practiced tricks and rode around the alleys near the shack for about an hour until it was lunchtime. My mind was focused on the cave the entire time. We agreed to meet back at the shack after lunch to repair Jimbo's surfboard, since he was due back from his grandparent's farm soon. I had never patched up a surfboard before.

Oz insisted it was not complicated. "He's going to join us soon. Let's repair it for him. I'll show you how to fix dings. It's easy."

When I arrived home the aroma of fish and sizzling bacon filled my nose as I entered the kitchen. My mom had prepared leftover seafood chowder and BLT sandwiches. I inhaled my meal like a wild animal, afterwards thanking my mom with a big hug before leaving to meet my friend again.

Still gorged and feeling a little drowsy, I leisurely walked my bike back to our private hideout. Oz already had Jimbo's surfboard resting on two sawhorses in the alley behind Nana's house.

"Are you ready for Surfboard Ding Repair 101?" Oz inquired as he rounded the corner with a brown cardboard box in his hand.

"Sure," I responded, not really knowing what he was talking about.

"I learned how to do this when my surfboard got a crack in it. My dad helped me fix it. It's really easy." Oz declared confidently. "Jimbo will be able to surf with us when he returns." He added.

"That's if the ocean cooperates," I commented and reminded him: "We haven't had decent waves in ages. It's about time for some surfing. Skateboarding just isn't a good enough substitute for me."

Oz nodded in agreement, and then pulled a white surgical mask and piece of sandpaper out of the box. He positioned the protective mask over his nose and mouth. He tossed me a mask and motioned for me to put it on. As he began sanding the area over the crack in Jimbo's surfboard, a fine dust formed around his hands while the breeze carried the rest through the air.

"First you have to roughen up the area so that the new resin will adhere." His voice was muffled by the mask as he pulled a rag out of the box and wiped the dust away. Then he retrieved a white shiny material made of chunky woven threads.

"This is fiberglass cloth. We must cut a piece big enough to fit over the ding." Oz spoke lightly. With a pair of scissors, he precisely trimmed a long two-inch wide strip of the material. "Now we must tape the area surrounding the damage. That will keep the resin from oozing so we don't get solid drips that are bumpy and we'll have to sand down later." Oz instructed me while tossing the rag back into his ding repair box. He pulled out a roll of masking tape. He inspected the ding once more and then tore strips of tape affixing them several inches away from the damaged area, creating a barrier around it. Not knowing what was going on, I just stood back and observed. Oz then threw the cylinder of masking tape back in the box and pulled out a pint sized shiny can and a small plastic bottle. He unscrewed the lid of the metal container and reached for an empty glass jar.

"This is the resin," Oz advised while pouring some of the thick clear blue tinged liquid into the jar. He picked up the small white bottle and stirred the resin using a tongue depressor stick. Simultaneously, he mixed drops from the small white bottle into the solution. The toxic smell of the chemicals became overwhelming, quickly filling the air.

"Okay, now we have to act fast." Oz spread a layer of resin over the ding and then positioned the pre-cut piece of fiberglass cloth on the area. Then, he smeared more of the sticky stuff on top of the fiberglass, until the ding was completely sealed. The resin was smooth to the eye and was contained within the masking tape barrier. It looked cool! The epoxy that pooled with the resin created a new shell on Jimbo's surfboard.

"Now we wait," he said as he unearthed a Frisbee® from the box.

"What's that for?" I asked.

"To pass the time," he answered with a grin and tossed the disk at me.

We pitched the disk around for about five minutes and then returned to our project. Oz delicately touched the resin with his index finger. It had turned from a liquid to a gel. Gently, he picked at the edges of the masking tape barrier. He peeled back the tape, rolled it up in a ball, and threw it into the trash.

"Now we have a nice clean edge." Oz admired his work of art, stepping back so I could look.

A clear thick layer of hardening epoxy resin had formed where he applied the mixture. I could barely detect the texture of the fiberglass cloth, which had turned from snow white to clear as glass after being submerged in the resin. The potent chemical fumes had almost completely dissipated.

"The repair is still sticky and hasn't adequately solidified yet. Time for a few more tosses." Oz threw the flying disk. It landed next to my foot. I picked it up, and hurled it back at him.

Intrigued by the process I asked: "Is that all you have to do to fix a surfboard?"

Oz caught it, wound up, and flung the disk in my direction, while responding, "Yeah, all we have to do now is sand it down and add more resin to make it even."

I leaped for the disk and acknowledged, "I'll try to avoid it, but if I get a ding on my surfboard I won't worry so much next time."

"Yeah," Oz replied, "But hopefully you'll never damage your board because some repairs aren't this easy!"

I chucked the Frisbee® back at him. My throw was awkward and Oz had to sprint up the cement alley to catch it. Instead, it changed direction and came crashing down. He went to retrieve it. Just as I leapt for the next catch, POWW, out of nowhere I felt a firm push on my shoulder. It startled me as the spinning disk rose over my head and out of my reach. Surprised by the unexpected shove, I turned around to see Jimbo's ear to ear grin.

"Gotcha," he laughed. "Hey strangers, what are you guys doing?"

"Just a little ding repair." Oz walked towards us, as Jimbo examined the ding wordlessly. I felt a little worried at first, since we hadn't asked him before we started working on his surfboard.

"We didn't expect you to be back from your vacation for a few more days, so we thought we'd try to fix your board," I replied while shaking Jimbo's hand.

"Cool." Jimbo finally looked up from admiring the repair. "Thanks guys! Are there any waves? Let's go out and surf!" Jimbo exclaimed.

Oz and I both solemnly shook our heads.

"It's flat, but we've made a discovery we have to tell you about!" I burst out.

Just then, the gate of Nana's yard creaked open. She came out into the alley, and as usual was wearing a colorful dress with a white apron over it.

"Welcome home young man. I have some chocolate chip cookies, if you're not bored with them yet." Nana shuffled over to us and gave Jimbo a hug.

"Hi, Nana." We all chimed in like a chorus. Once again, Jimbo grabbed one too many cookies.

"It looks like you're doing fiberglass repairs. Make sure you wash those chemicals off your hands thoroughly when you're finished. I'll put a bar of soap by the garden faucet, and I think I'll leave it there for you boys. Then you can easily clean yourselves up when you get dirty from the yard work." Nana returned to the house proud of her idea.

After washing our hands thoroughly we ate the cookies and excitedly told Jimbo all about Turtle Cave, and in turn, we listened to his adventures at his Grandparents' farm. Once the epoxy was dry, we sanded down the bumps until they were smooth, and added one more coat of resin. When that finally dried, we sanded it again. Jimbo's board almost looked as good as new!

"Tomorrow, we explore Turtle Cave!" I exclaimed.

# CHAPTER 12
## The Shaft

I can't wait to see what you guys found!" Jimbo roared as we stood at the high cliff looking down at the sea.

Turtle Cave was not visible from our standpoint, so Oz pointed from the top of the bluff to show Jimbo the direction in which we were headed.

"I think today will be a great day!" Jimbo proclaimed, posturing dangerously near the edge of the cliff as if he were great army general. It was comical that our self-elected leader didn't know where to go.

The tide had made its exodus, so we had no choice but to walk through some deeper water in the tide pools before we arrived at the cave. Paddling on our surfboards was not an option. The water level was so low that the exposed reef and rock would have ruined our boards. We hiked most of the way. It helped that we were wearing shoes.

Once we arrived at the cave, we waded though its open mouth slowly maneuvering through the still ocean. Jimbo was silent for once, with awe. As we reached the ridge inside the cave, we climbed up and dropped our gear. Oz put his makeshift flashlight helmet on his head and switched it on. A beam of light hit the cave wall and brightened the entire chamber.

"I think we should bring our surfboards into the passage so there's no chance of them washing away with the tide." I advised.

"Good idea." Oz approved.

"We can stand them up in the dry area of the cavern. That way we know for sure our boards won't disappear if the tide returns and waves come crashing back." Oz chuckled, while he cautiously scaled over the boulder pile and gently placed his surfboard down before climbing through the jagged opening in the soaked wooden door.

"Hey Buzz, hand me the boards." He commanded.

I scaled over the heap and angled my surfboard to fit through the entrance, then handed it to Oz and waited while he placed mine a few yards back in the chamber. Jimbo climbed over the boulders and lingered next to me. Oz returned and I passed him his surfboard.

"I'll carry my own board," Jimbo snapped as I reached out for it.

Shrugging my shoulders, ignoring his usual impatience, I turned my flashlight on and climbed between the metal bars attached to the door. Jimbo followed closely behind me into the dark tunnel.

"Okay, we have two hours to explore before our batteries run out of juice, but the tide will change in about an hour and we will have to turn back then." Oz spoke confidently as he resumed the lead.

We followed the chalk symbols on the walls that marked our previous expedition, and walked silently, single file. Jimbo gazed around in amazement as he trailed Oz, and I was at the back of the line.

"Hi-ho, hi-ho," Jimbo sang as we joined with whistling. Our trio echoed shrill sounds throughout the cave. Arriving at another access to the passage, we discontinued our harmony. The tunnel was now only five feet high. Oz ducked and crouched down. Jimbo pursued. I felt a little uneasy and took a deep gulp of air before following my friends. We made slower progress walking crouched. As we advanced further through the tunnel, its ceiling steadily got higher until we were able to walk upright once again. After a few more yards, we entered a large chamber. At first we were disappointed, thinking we had reached a dead end. Shining our flashlights against the far wall of the cavern, we observed a strange rusty wheel. It was attached to the cave wall by an equally rusty metal bracket. We stood next to each other aiming our flashlights on it.

"It looks like a pulley," Oz hypothesized and then directed his beam of light straight upwards. "And this shaft; it looks man-made. Hey, there's another pulley up in the ceiling," he added.

The vertical shaft was perfectly square and there were metal re-bar prongs protruding from inside of its cement wall to create a ladder. Another rusty wheel hung high above us. The chamber wasn't a dead end after all. The connecting passage was elevated about fifteen feet above us, and at the top of the ladder was a ledge.

"I see a route up there." I pointed.

"Yeah," Jimbo agreed. "We must move onward and upward, otherwise, we're going to be stuck."

Jimbo aimed the beam of his flashlight up and shined it in the direction we wanted to scale. I had trouble climbing trees so this task seemed impossible. The three of us stood in a half circle staring up at the shaft and makeshift ladder pointing our flashlights toward our destination above.

"This shouldn't be too challenging," Oz assessed. "Someone must have used this cave often enough to go through all the effort of cementing the wall and constructing a pulley mechanism." He elaborated on his theory.

"How do we get up there?" I inquired with reservation, already knowing the answer to my own question.

"The two of you will boost me up into the chamber and I'll tie a rope to the ladder. Then we can climb up." Oz directed.

Jimbo nodded with approval and added: "Perfect idea."

Oz swung the bag off his shoulder and retrieved some climbing rope.

"You guys hoist me up." He commanded.

Jimbo and I nervously stared at each other in the dim light. Oz positioned the beam of his flashlight on the ground, propping it up on a nearby stone so that it illuminated the wall he was about to scale. He then strapped his hard-hat helmet with an attached light to his head.

"I'm ready for battle," he declared as he gave us a military salute.

Jimbo and I stood next to Oz, who clamped the end of the rope between his teeth and began climbing by grabbing hold of cracks in the wall. We helped to boost him up until he could stand on Jimbo's shoulders. Oz's helmet fell off of his head and grazed the side of Jimbo's head.

"Ouch!" Jimbo whined.

"Hold still, I've almost got it." Oz hissed in response.

"Alright," Jimbo exhaled impatiently.

Suddenly, Oz's feet rose up into the ghostly shaft. The lower end of the rope wiggled and swung back and forth as he advanced higher.

"Hey, tie my helmet to the rope so I can pull it up." Oz ordered. Jimbo performed exactly as our comrade instructed and replied, "Reel it up!"

The rope and the helmet with the taped-on flashlight disappeared into the black cavity above us. Our beams weren't powerful enough to spot Oz, and a peaceful silence filled the chamber as we waited. After a few minutes which seemed like an eternity, a burst of welcome light blasted through the tunnel and the rope came plummeting back down and smacked on the ground.

"Climb up." Oz commanded from above.

Without asking who should go next, Jimbo lodged the strap of his flashlight between his teeth, pushed his way in front of me, and snatched the rope. He tugged on it and then tested the line by hanging on it with his legs bent. It held his weight sufficiently and he dropped to his feet again. Jimbo jumped up and clutched the rope about a foot over his head. Using his feet to support himself against the wall, he pulled himself up and disappeared into the passage overhead. I was overwhelmed with the feeling of butterflies in my stomach because it was my turn. Impressed with both my friends' climbing abilities, I hoped to have enough muscle to scale the wall. I grasped the rope and attempted to walk up the shaft like Jimbo. My struggle failed as my feet slipped down the damp concrete and my hands smoldered with rope burn. Out of strength, I dropped to the floor. I tried again and again, but failed each time. My feet continued to slither down the wall and my arms neglected to drag me up. A tinge of anger surged through my body as I heard my friends giggling from overhead.

"You need help getting up here, Buzz? Do we need to bring a special ladder for you next time?" Jimbo teased.

The last question pierced me like a dart. I felt self-conscious and humiliated.

"It's safe, don't worry," Oz attempted to reassure me. I wasn't sure how sincere my friend was, though.

By now my face was blazing hot and I was glad the light was dim because I was sure my cheeks were beet red. "ARRGGHHH!" Giving it my all, I seized the rope above my head and dug my feet into a groove in the wall as my arms pulled the rest of my body up the rope. When I approached the first step of the rebar ladder, I released my right hand from the rope and grabbed the cold metal. There was a feeling of roughness from the rust on my hands. Oh, no! My sweaty palms began to slide from the bar. I dug the toes of my soaking wet tennis shoes into a crevice, released the rope, and reached as high up the ladder as possible. I gripped a higher rung and then heaved up reaching for the next with my other hand, finally planting both feet on the lowest rung. Feeling secure on the ladder, I captured a deep swallow of air and exhaled exuberantly.

"Whew," I exclaimed catching my breath!

"Hold tight," I heard Jimbo from above as I took one careful step at a time up the shaft.

Oz was already off the ladder looking down at us from the ledge above. His grin shined in the faint light. When Jimbo cleared the top of the ladder, Oz helped him onto the ledge. Following cautiously, I made my way to the ridge. The shelf was about eight feet wide, and twenty feet away was an additional stone wall.

"Right-on, you made it!" Oz slapped me on the shoulder and then extended his hand. I grabbed it and he assisted me off the ladder, over the ledge onto the platform. It was unmistakably constructed by a person because the edges were much smoother than the walls near the ocean entrance.

"Check it out, there's another corridor!" Jimbo shouted a few feet ahead of us. "Over here," his voice echoed throughout the rock cavern.

Oz hastily chased Jimbo, and I tagged along carefully, attempting not to leave much space between us. We trailed him through a passageway.

Instinctively I deliberated out loud: "Hey, what if we can't find our way out of the cave? We haven't marked our trail with an 'X' or an arrow in a while."

Jimbo paused and held his flashlight under his chin shining the light straight up on his face, giving himself a monster-like appearance.

Ignoring his shenanigans I persisted: "Hey Oz, we've journeyed a long time underground. Should we make sure to mark our way back."

"If we were Hansel & Gretel, we could use bread," Jimbo retorted cynically.

"Yeah, but the birds ate their marker. We don't have to worry about that, because I've got chalk. We'll mark this spot." Oz announced.

Pulling a thick stick of white chalk from his waist belt, Oz drew a big arrow on the wall of the passage. It pointed in the direction we had come from.

Jimbo continued onward. As we paced, Oz marked the wall with arrows pointing back to the shaft at regular intervals like he did on our last visit to the cave. Trekking further into the tunnel, a muffled BEEP BEEP BEEP BEEP BEEP BEEP BEEP BEEP BEEP, could be heard. Oz had set the timer on the watch Nana gave him to prevent us from being trapped in the cavern when the tide rose. Because of the extreme high and low tides on this day, missing the tide could mean waiting in the cold murky cave for almost three hours. Only when the tide turned and let us go from its dreary cavern, would we be free again.

"Time to go." Oz announced. "We have more battery power, but the tide is coming up."

"Aw, shhh!," Jimbo hissed. He could not hide his disappointment, while I concealed my relief. I really didn't feel comfortable going further and welcomed the prospect of returning to the warm sunlight.

"Just when we are actually getting somewhere, we have to stop our expedition and turn back." Jimbo complained, but nevertheless, followed us back to the ledge and the rebar ladder. I went first, Jimbo was last. Before descending the ladder Jimbo informed us: "I'll leave the rope here, so we can climb right up. Maybe we need to bring a step-stool for Buzz next time." He continued to poke fun at me. Jimbo displayed a superior arrogance while cackling in the subtle glow of our flashlights. We walked wordlessly, single file towards the entrance of the tunnel. I felt ashamed and irritated to be reminded of my difficulty climbing the rope.

Jimbo changed the subject by whistling: "Hi-ho, hi-ho."

Oz joined in, and of course shortly after, I did too, and we chuckled and whistled all the way back to the entrance of the cave. We easily reached the wooden door. After retrieving our boards, we exited. The morning was still bright and I was forced to narrow my eyes to a squint as we paddled our surfboards back into the open world. The transition felt strange and it took a while for my sight to adjust to the sky's illumination. Outside the cave, I tore off my soggy shoes and rash guard and hoisted my gear bag and surfboard up onto a dry boulder. I waded through the tepid water surrounding the rock. My feet sunk into the soft sand, the water surface glistened in the brilliant summer sun.

"I'm going for a swim," I notified my friends, with the water up to my knees. I was still feeling a little sore about Jimbo teasing me. The crystal clear ocean invited me further.

When I reached the rock's shelf, green sea grass gave way to burgundy moss that encrusted the rocks at its edge to the deep azure ocean. I leapt off of the shallow ledge and dove in. Underwater, I stretched out my arms in front of me and cupped my hands, plunging deeper through the ocean until I felt its pressure pushing on my eardrums. The grit and slime from the cave washed away from my body. The ocean felt soothing. Clearing more distance, I challenged myself with a few more arm strokes. As the urge to breathe overwhelmed my lungs, I torpedoed up to the water surface and gulped fresh air. I spotted my buddies about thirty yards from the ledge. They were wading from the large boulder in my direction. Swimming towards them, Oz and Jimbo plummeted off the shelf into the crystal blue water. I submerged once again. The ocean was so clear that Oz and Jimbo were visible splashing in the distance.

I popped up out of the sea. "Wow, the ocean is tremendously clear today," I announced as the salt water ran from my eyes. Our party treaded in place.

"If the tide is too high to explore the cave, we should return to the beach after lunch for some snorkeling. I'll bring my spear gun." Jimbo was eager to give the fish hunt another try.

"Unfortunately, I can't. As a matter of fact I need to run now, or I'll be late," Oz replied after glancing at his watch raising his eyebrows.

"Well you better learn to run on water Oz, because you're already late." Jimbo snidely retorted, but was ignored.

Jimbo and I decided to return to the same spot and go snorkeling later that afternoon. He suggested asking my mom if he could come to my house for lunch, and I agreed. We trailed behind Oz, who was already rapidly swimming back to the beach. We retrieved our gear and ascended up the bluff to our bikes. Oz was hurriedly uncovering the camouflage branches as we emerged. He quickly unlocked his chain and disentangled it from our bicycles.

"I have to hurry home," Oz panted out of breath. Jimbo and I watched our friend rush off.

# CHAPTER 13
## Stinks Like Fish

Jimbo came over to my house, and naturally, Mom invited him for lunch before I could say anything. Afterwards, we hung out in my bedroom, read surf magazines, and watched a DVD on the History of Surfing. Following a few hours of relaxation, we headed off to the shack and picked up our snorkeling gear and Jimbo's spear gun.

"I've got a new piece of equipment," he announced proudly.

Jimbo opened his backpack and pulled out a shiny new diver's knife. The rubber straps on the sheath wiggled as he displayed it to me proudly. He removed the thick black fastener and yanked the yellow handle, drawing the knife from its sheath. The blade was wide and the opposite side had a serrated edge resembling a miniature saw. Jimbo smiled as I peered at the blade in awe. He presented it to me. I clenched its plastic handle, and it was bulky and felt awkward in my grip, most definitely heavier than a kitchen knife.

"This is the bomb!" I exclaimed.

"Yeah, my Grandpa bought me this blade at a sport's department store. But I had to clean out a lot of horse stables to earn it. He even taught me knife safety," Jimbo admitted sternly. I passed the knife with the blade pointing at him.

"Ah, no that's not how you hand someone a knife safely, duh!" Jimbo switched into his bossy mode as he seized the knife by its sharp end snorting arrogantly.

"Let's go," I managed to ignore him.

When we returned to the ocean, the tide was high and the sea blanketed the reefs and rocks that had been exposed that morning. There was not a cloud in the sky, so the sun's rays penetrated deep down and the visibility seemed at least a hundred feet under the sea. It was the most transparent water we had ever witnessed. Jimbo swam ahead of me with the spear gun poised. I took a more leisurely course. To be honest, I didn't think he had a chance of spearing a fish or for that matter, even getting close enough to one. Whenever he shot the gun at a group of fish, they would playfully swim around the approaching spear. Jimbo kicked even further ahead of me with his fins, and I followed. Instead of swimming on the surface though, I dove down six feet and swam below. We took a quick turn towards a rock that had been partially exposed at low tide. Jimbo yanked the knife from the sheath which was fastened to his left calf. He located a boulder and used his blade to chip away at the rock under water.

Out of the blue, a massive school of tiny two-inch turquoise and silver fish darted in front of me. I swam towards them as they flashed away. They looked like a swarm of bees. I followed the shiny fish, and every movement of my body resulted in a startled reaction from the school, especially when I reached out to touch one. The living cloud of fish moved like one creature. I pursued it as fast as my fins would propel me. As the immense cluster finally dissipated and swam out of my reach, the chasing game became monotonous. I searched around under water, but Jimbo was out of sight. His snorkel became easily visible when a strip of bright orange tape around the tip bobbed out of the ocean about fifty feet away from me. I started leisurely kicking towards Jimbo with my fins, still fatigued from our morning adventure into Turtle Cave. My pace was listless, and my attention was on the sea floor. Occasionally, I would pause when I encountered something interesting to examine it closer. Some pumpkin colored starfish appeared, and a small octopus scurried under a rock, but my journey was mainly uneventful around the emerald grass and soaring amber seaweed.

I peeked up to see Jimbo's head and snorkel at the same spot where I left him. A humongous school of pan-sized metallic fish darted towards him. Jimbo's pale, blurry body and yellow swim trunks came into focus as I zoomed closer. The school of fish was whirling around the area he had hacked with his new knife. The horde began picking at the rock as if they didn't see him. I slowed my pace and then quit kicking altogether with my fins delicately gliding along the sea's surface. Jimbo and the mass of ravenous fish were only ten feet ahead of me. He hoisted the spear gun pointing it at the fish, which were plucking at the rocks with their tiny jagged teeth. Hiding behind a boulder, I attentively observed my friend as he arched his back and aimed the spear's tip at the crowd of fish. He pulled the trigger and the gun discharged like a rocket. To my astonishment, the spear hit its target! A single fish wriggled helplessly at the end of the sharp point. The plate sized fish sunk to the bottom with the spear wedged in its side, its tail flapping. Needless to say, the rest of the school desperately fled from the scene as their comrade's fate clung to the end of Jimbo's spear gun. A primeval feeling of excitement overcame me as Jimbo signed, THUMBS UP, under the water. He held the spear and his trophy over his head with elation.

We hurriedly swam towards one another. I spat out my snorkel and exclaimed, "Wow! Jimbo you got one!" My friend smiled triumphantly.

"I smashed a couple of mussels with my knife and watched for the fish to come and feed. And then, POW! I bagged this one!" Jimbo exclaimed.

With a jubilant smile, my friend's diving mask rested on his forehead with the snorkel dangling on the side of his left ear. An oval red suction mark surrounded his eyebrows and upper lip from the mask as he carted the fish on his spear above the water.

"Let's head in," Jimbo suggested euphorically. We waded to the shore, and he used his special knife to pry the fish off of the spear.

"Okay, now let's hurry back to my house before this thing rots." Jimbo ordered as he placed the fish in a plastic grocery bag.

After we raced back to the shack and rinsed our gear, we hopped on our bikes and hustled over to Jimbo's place. No one was home when we arrived.

"Wait here, I'll unlock the gate." He commanded while scrambling up a tree that grew next to his house and over the fence of their well-kept yard. A few minutes later, I heard him running back to the entrance with his keys jingling. The padlock clicked, and then the gate swung open.

"Come on in," Jimbo gestured with his hand.

We pulled our bikes into the yard. Jimbo marched over to the garden hose on the side of the small cottage.

"We have to clean it first." Jimbo educated me as he unraveled the plastic bag and pulled out the fish carcass. Its big, glassy, round eyes stared at me. I felt sorry for it lying there. Jimbo's portly gray and black striped cat, Becker, clawed his way over the neighbor's fence.

"Meow!" Becker greeted Jimbo with a munchkin's roar and then turned to me when his master ignored him. He was too focused on his trophy to notice. As my friend tossed the slimy grocery bag onto the grass, the enormous Bengal cat instantly pounced over to the sack and inspected it. The tip of Becker's tail twitched back and forth with curiosity and excitement. Jimbo held the fish with his left index finger inside the gill as he turned on the water. The odor of the kill in his owner's hand was stimulating enough to bypass Becker's fear and loathing of the water. He purred brashly and tilted his striped body against Jimbo's left leg. My friend cleaned the fish meticulously, rinsing its slippery body under the hose's trickling stream. When Jimbo was satisfied, he crouched down and patted Becker on the head. The huge cat let out a desperate, MMMEEEEOOOWWWW, while begging for his master's catch.

"Aw, come on Becker, get lost!" Jimbo hissed.

The cat scurried away, and Jimbo took a deep breath as he poked the knife's point at the fish's belly. The blade was too dull and it slipped off of the fish. Jimbo tried again. This time the carcass slipped out of his hands and into his mother's rose bush. He was getting frustrated.

"I'm going into the kitchen to get another knife," he asserted in a determined tone. "Buzz, get the fish so Becker doesn't rip his claws into it." My friend ordered.

Jimbo left me poking around for his trophy in a thorny plant while he went to retrieve a more suitable filleting tool. I stared down at the prize, and its scales sparkled like tiny prisms in the afternoon sun. Moments later, my buddy returned with a pointy kitchen knife.

"This will work." Jimbo's confidence was renewed.

I tossed him the fish; scales now covered my hands, too. Jimbo crouched down in the grass and tightly held the catch in his grasp. The blade penetrated the belly of the fish with ease, and he made a skillful incision. Bloody guts and other grizzly components oozed from its body. It made me nauseous.

"Man, that's gross!" I resounded.

"Yeah, you'll get used to it. My Grandpa took me fishing every day during my visit, except for Sundays. Then my Grandma made me dress up and go to church with her." Jimbo revealed as he sprayed the inside of the fish with clean water from the hose. "A couple times we camped out and cooked the fish over a fire. Today, you are in for a culinary treat, buddy." He raved. "Now that I've separated the guts, next come the gills, and then we'll remove the scales." Jimbo continued.

Judging by the number of flakes already on his hands, face and shirt, it didn't seem like there could be anymore left. He used the blade of the knife to scrape off the remainder of the fish scales under the running water.

"Here, you try the other side," he encouraged handing me the fish and the knife.

The task was straightforward, and the blade made scratching sounds as the scales sloughed off the carcass. As I finished, Jimbo doused the fish and the knife with more water. Becker was overjoyed and purred as we passed him on our way into the house. I peered back and watched him leisurely approach the fish guts we had abandoned on the drenched lawn.

We entered the small cottage where Jimbo and his mom lived, passing through the backdoor. Jimbo placed the fish into the kitchen sink and pulled down a frying pan that was hanging on a pot rack above the stove. He turned on the gas burner which, click-click-click-clicked, until the flame ignited.

"Ah yez, ze butta," Jimbo joked with a French accent as he held the refrigerator door open with his foot. 'Chef Jimbo' unwrapped an entire stick of butter and lobbed it into the warm skillet. Its long rectangular form melted into a fluid puddle within seconds. At first, the familiar pleasant smell of mild butter filled the air. Jimbo then tended to the fish in the sink.

The butter in the frying pan started sizzling and splattering all over the stovetop. The kitchen gradually became fogged up with smoke, and I began to doubt if my friend knew what he was doing.

"Hey Jimbo, this looks like a problem." I urged, staring at the frying pan.

I didn't really know how to cook, but smoke billowing from the grease seemed wrong. Ignoring my concern, Jimbo proceeded to hum a tune as he rubbed salt on the fish. Nevertheless, the smoky smell converted into a thick gray canopy around the stove.

"Okay, time for some heat!" Jimbo held the fish in one hand and grabbed the smoldering frying pan in the other. He plopped the body onto its charred surface. The loud, TZZZZ, of the fish sizzling on the hot skillet erupted into a flickering plume of fire rising up from the pan. My eyes were stinging and I began feverishly hacking as the entire kitchen filled up with fumes. I opened a window and stepped toward the backdoor as my friend squeezed lemon juice over the fish. Jimbo coughed wildly after inhaling the harsh exhaust billowing from the stove. It was starting to look as if he really didn't know what he was doing.

"Asseeztant pleeze hand me zee spat-ula, over there, quick!" He shouted pointing insistently.

Jimbo ceased speaking in his French chef accent. Now, he looked more like a mad scientist standing over an experiment gone awry. I grabbed the spatula from a hook under the cupboard and handed it to him. He stabbed at the side of the fish with the wide tip but it stuck to the skillet. Smoke continued to fill the kitchen.

"Darn, we need non-stick pans! How can I work with inferior equipment?" Jimbo gestured by brandishing the spatula over his head, waving through the thick black smoke.

"JAMES DONOVAN MURPHY!" Jimbo froze as an angry female voice belted. Jimbo turned pale. His mother was standing in the doorway as the sun reflected behind her frizzled bleach blond hair. She looked as if she just had been electrocuted. Her oversized fur purse weighted over her shoulder and both arms embraced brown paper grocery bags. She appeared furious. The look of terror on Jimbo's mug didn't help my extreme anxiety.

"IT SMELLS LIKE A BURNT FISH MARKET IN HERE!" She screamed and targeted her glare at me. An unfriendly chill ran down my spine.

"You had better go home now, Buzz." Jimbo's mother snarled. She horrified me at first, but I was relieved to be excused from the impending scene. Jimbo's mom focused her infuriated stare back on my friend.

"Good luck," I waved at Jimbo reassuringly and noticed an array of colorful fish scales glued to the back of my hand.

My friend solemnly nodded his sweaty brow. We both knew his looming fate would be that of a condemned prisoner. To add insult to injury, the smoke detector in the hall pierced through the entire house. The noise throbbed in my ears as I rushed out the back door, grateful to be leaving.

Once outside, I could hear every sound blasting from the cottage. The stench of the curdled smoke was now billowing out of the opened window.

"TURN OFF THE STOVE. WHAT'S THE BIG IDEA?" Jimbo's mom slammed open the side window.

As I tip-toed through the yard, I cringed for my friend. Becker the big Bengal cat waited for me on the pathway licking his paws. He obliged me with a loud, PURRRRRRRRR, as if he was offering gratitude for the fish guts we left for him.

Ms. Murphy's yelling tapered and the smoke dissipated as I pedaled further away from Jimbo's house.

Later that evening I received a call. It was brief: "Hey Buzz, I can only talk for a minute, my mom just ran to the neighbor's house. I'm grounded until Saturday." Jimbo's voice whispered miserably. He continued to mumble into the telephone receiver. "And worst of all, I have to go to my mother's hair-salon and assist her at work all week!"

"It was the kitchen inferno, huh?" I asked.

"Yeah, that and a few other things she discovered in my bedroom while she was on her rampage," he admitted. "Don't explore the cave until I can come too, okay?" He pleaded.

"Sure," I promised.

"She's back, time to go!" Jimbo hurriedly added before he abruptly hung up.

Poor guy, I thought, of course we'll postpone our adventure. Naturally, Oz agreed too.

# CHAPTER 14
## A New Corridor

Unfortunately for Jimbo, a fun swell hit the coast the first day of his week long punishment. Consistent two to three foot waves blessed our beaches. Oz and I could abstain from exploring Turtle Cave until Jimbo's restriction ended, but asking us to stay out of the ocean was unthinkable. Loyal to our buddy's request, we delayed our expedition into Turtle Cave and enjoyed great surfing without our friend.

"We probably couldn't even get into the cave anyway. Waves are breaking inside the reef," Oz commented.

"Oh yeah, I almost forgot what happened when the breakers hit the cave during one of our first missions!" I imagined what it would be like in the cavern during a big swell. "Dangerous" would be an understatement. After we enjoyed a summer morning of surfing, Oz and I parted ways. I had to return home by noon, and Oz promised to help his dad install a new toilet in their guest bathroom.

On my way back, I remembered my defeating, humiliating experience in the cave. I had temporarily forgotten how rotten I had felt, and I decided to search for some rope in the garage. My eyes had difficulty adjusting to the low light of the garage interior. I flipped on the light switch and a pair of fluorescent tubes buzzed above me. They flickered then barely brightened the area. I dug through a few old boxes. Some contained vintage clothes, used books, and even several of my dad's rowing trophies from college. The best item I could find was clothesline. That wouldn't work, I thought to myself. Glancing up toward the rafters in the ceiling, I noticed my dad's old sailboat had some extra rope that draped from its sail! I grabbed the ladder and pried it apart, then scrambled up and climbed onto the rafters. The rope was still attached to the mast of the sailboat, and I knew my dad wouldn't appreciate me dismantling it. Staring down at the oil stained garage floor, I imagined myself scaling the rope with ease and didn't want to be the laughing stock ever again. I lost myself in thought about our adventure through Turtle Cave, and wondered how our discovery would end. I snapped back to reality when I heard my little brother's piercing screams coming from his bedroom. I'd better hurry, Mom won't be too happy with me up here. Just as I headed for the ladder, I felt lucky when I discovered ropes of varying sizes in a blue plastic milk crate, hiding under a tarp behind the boat. I found the perfect piece to practice climbing! It was easily over fifty feet long and delicately frayed. Could a mouse have chewed on it? I dropped the rope down to the garage floor, and quickly followed. It was almost identical to the one Oz brought to the cave, and long enough for me to cut to my desired length.

The mature gnarled redwood tree in our yard had a bulky branch that grew out horizontally. It was a cinch to climb. Sometimes when I was angry or sad or just wanted to be alone, climbing up that old tree helped me ponder my problems. I scaled its trunk and tied one end of the rope to a branch so that it hung down about three feet from the base. Then I leaped back down, yanking at the line to ensure that it would hold my mass. I jumped up the rope and clenched it with both hands. With my knees bent, I swung around in a circle several times.

The knot still held tight with all of my weight. I told myself: "You can do this." Yanking on the rope with my left hand and reaching up with the right, I alternated in that sequence to scale the line higher each time.

"Argh!" I groaned with each pull toward the top. My palms were sweaty and raw. Halfway up, my hands began to slip. I clamped the rope between my feet, but my burning fingers couldn't take the friction any longer. To escape further pain, I dropped onto the lawn below.

"Hi, Buzz," I heard my dad's voice from behind me. He had just arrived home from work. "Time for dinner," he smiled as he looked up at the rope. "Practicing climbing?" He asked.

"Hoping to reach the top," I answered while looking up toward the tree clasping my blistered hands together. Even though the urge was strong, I stopped myself from telling him why I was training.

The next morning I tried to go up the rope again. The first two attempts were worse than my experience in the cave. During my third effort, I reminisced about my last trip to the zoo, and how the monkeys swiftly maneuvered their bodies up and down the trees with grace and ease. I imagined myself doing the same, and suddenly, I was getting it! Before I knew it, I had climbed fifteen feet above ground. I was proud of myself, but I knew more practice was needed to overpower the rope in the cave. My thoughts were interrupted when my brain realized that my arms and hands didn't have the strength to hold on to the rope anymore. I rapidly slid down the line like a fireman. THUMP, my feet plopped down on the lumpy grass. I had some serious rope burn. "Yes!" I cheered. It was a small success, but I knew that I was closer to accomplishing my goal.

The rest of the morning was spent running errands with my mom and watching my little brother. We went to the grocery store and loaded up the shopping cart with food and other goodies. At least the market wasn't as grueling for me as the mall! I still couldn't wait to get back home though, with thoughts of early afternoon waves rolling through my head. After helping Mom unload the car, I folded up the paper shopping bags and grabbed a leftover sandwich from the fridge. Looking at my mom and without me uttering a word, she responded almost as if she was a psychic that could read my mind.

"Okay, be back before dinner time, Buzz." She instructed.

The telephone at Oz's house went unanswered, so I hopped on my bike and rode down to the beach with the bologna sandwich clenched in my mouth. The swell from the previous day had dropped significantly, and the waves were measly and blown out. The temperature had become a little cooler, too. I didn't have the urge to surf and Oz wasn't at the shack, so I enjoyed a nice leisurely bike ride back home. The rest of the day was spent practicing rope climbing. After dinner, I got a call from Jimbo.

"Hey Buzz, I'm finally off restriction. Tomorrow we can go back to the cave and explore!" Jimbo's excitement was contagious.

"Terrific! I'll be ready at dawn." I interrupted, but Jimbo corrected me.

"Oz insisted we should go in the late afternoon because of the tide. Let's meet at the shack at three o'clock." He paused.

"I'll have to check with my parents first." I told him.

I was worried about getting left out of the adventure exploring the cave. My mother said it was okay to go hangout with my friends at the new skateboard park by the city athletic fields. There was never any mention of crawling and climbing around in an ocean cave. Otherwise, her answer would have been a big "NO!"

Just as we planned, Oz, Jimbo and I met at the shack at three o'clock the very next afternoon. Nana looked happy as she passed us wearing a fancy dress, hat and gloves. Her big bag was hanging over her arm.

"I'm late for a dinner party, boys. Be good." She got in her huge, dusty, black car that was always parked in the alley, and opened the door which creaked loudly. After two failed attempts the classic sedan started with a loud boom. Nana waved as she putted off. I felt glad that our trio was finally together again. We chattered throughout our entire journey down to the water and our voices boomed with laughter as we paddled into the cave's mouth. The tide was already at its lowest point.

"I think we should store our surfboards in the cave so there's no chance of them getting swept away." I suggested.

"Good idea." Oz agreed.

"We can haul 'em with us and shelter them in the cavern's dry area. That way we know for sure they won't disappear." Oz chuckled, while he pulled his flashlight helmet out of his backpack. He advanced toward the boulder pile and slowly climbed over it, gently placing his surfboard down next to the entrance. Like a mouse, he scurried through the metal bars in the door's face, and slid deeper into the cave's darkness.

"Hey Buzz, hand me the boards." Oz said reaching out his hand.

I climbed over the mound and handed him our surfboards, one by one, as Oz gently stood them up a few yards further in the chamber. Jimbo followed scrambling over the boulders, and we maneuvered past the metal bars. The glow on Oz's hardhat lit the passageway for us, and we had to sprint twenty yards to catch up with him.

"Hurry up, slow pokes." Oz urged us on with laughter.

Our troop hiked down the passage following our previous chalk marks, which led us to the dome shaped cavern. Climbing up the rope was a cinch. This time, thanks to my practice at home, I pulled myself up to the ladder and made it over the ledge with ease. We continued to track our chalk marks until we reached the final arrow Oz had drawn on the wall during our last exploration. We were surveying new territory. The three of us trailed through the stone corridor until it lead us to another, larger crevice. The new fissure was about ten feet high and three feet wide. We stood in the center of the chamber and shined our flashlights around the jagged ceiling and stone walls. There were two additional openings on the opposite end of the chamber from where we had entered. Oz pulled a piece of chalk out of his backpack and drew arrows on both sides of the route pointing to where we had come from. We sure didn't want to get lost and take the wrong path back! Jimbo directed the beam of his flashlight back and forth, from one of the new channel openings to the other.

"Eenie meenie mynee mo, through which portal shall we go?" Jimbo smirked.

"I'm not sure," I responded reluctantly.

"We should just go through one passage, and see where it leads. Then we'll follow our trail back and explore the next one." Oz answered with determination.

"I sure don't think that we should split up," my vote was for staying together.

"Well, I think that we should choose..." Jimbo spoke with a ghostly shrill, paused, and then shined his flashlight swiftly from one passage entrance to the other.

"Door Number Two!" He roared. Oz and I remained silent.

Jimbo's voice ricocheted through the cave as he pointed the beam of his flashlight on the entrance of the cleft to our right. He disappeared into the cavity and we hurried after him. We walked in a single file line down the route for approximately twenty yards. But to our dismay, the cavern turned out to be a dead end. Jimbo reached the end of the corridor first, and patted the palms of his hands against the solid rock barrier.

"That won't budge." He declared, forcing his bodyweight and thrusting his shoulders against the stone wall. "About face, and forward march!" Jimbo commanded, imitating an army drill sergeant.

We turned around as we retraced our steps and followed the glow of Oz's flashlight until we were back in the large familiar cavern. Oz immediately took the lead walking into the remaining unexplored passage. Jimbo pushed his way in front of me, chasing at Oz's heels. I didn't leave much space between my two friends either. A balmy chill ran up my vertebrae and I felt a strange tinge of fear. The atmosphere suddenly became much warmer. Sweat dripped from my forehead. Instead of ending abruptly after a short distance like the previous chasm, this route made a sharp left bend. The beams of Oz and Jimbo's flashlights vanished around the corner. Suddenly alone, wondering if they were in some sort of a race, I sprinted to catch up. The tunnel was much darker with just my flashlight to illuminate its corridors. It was a relief to turn the corner and see my friends.

"I wonder how far above sea-level we've traveled?" I asked, catching my breath.

"Definitely twenty stories up," Jimbo answered authoritatively. "Maybe even a thousand feet," he added.

"That's a little extreme. Maybe we're four stories up," Oz disagreed.

The passage stretched for another fifty yards and steadily inclined as we traveled through a maze of narrow chambers.

"Hey there's a door up ahead!" Oz broke his silence with an excited outburst.

"Perhaps the treasure chamber is right behind it." I added with anticipation.

"We'll have to figure out how to spend all of the riches. First I'm gonna purchase my mom a big house." Jimbo chattered with glee.

"We can buy the entire surf shop!" I burst out with animation. The thought of owning all of those shiny brand new surfboards was electrifying.

"But how do we get the door open? That is the million dollar question." Oz brought us back to reality.

For several minutes, we stood next to each other silently shining the beams from our flashlights onto the metal door. I had no brilliant ideas, and my friends hadn't a clue either, so I jokingly said: "We could drive an ax into it."

"That will take a long time; this door is made out of metal." Oz replied.

"Hey what if we picked the lock? We'd probably have to get the locksmith who helped open that chest for us." Jimbo sounded serious.

"Yeah, what are we going to say to him? 'Hey Mister, can you swim to a cave and hike around in a mysterious cavern to help us unlock a secret door?'" I mockingly remarked. Jimbo glared at me, rolling his eyes. Oz ignored us both. The construction helmet that he had affixed his flashlight to was resting slightly tilted on his head. He remained silent lost deep in thought with his eyebrows raised and his forehead wrinkled.

"I have a plan," Oz finally erupted. He pulled his backpack off, dropped it at his feet and unzipped it. "Here, hold my flashlight." Oz handed it to Jimbo. He proceeded to yank a hammer and a large screwdriver out of his backpack.

"Maybe I can undo the hinges and we can pry the door open," Oz said.

He approached the hatch and began tapping the handle of the screwdriver as he held its point under the bottom hinge. CLING…CLING…CLING, beating the metal hinge with a screwdriver sounded like an old school bell. After several hard blows, the top of the bolt began to pop out above the hinge. Oz continued working as Jimbo and I remained in the background, mesmerized by our friend's ingenuity. At last, he finished until each bolt was sticking up about a half an inch above the four separate hinges.

"Okay, I think this may work." Oz stepped back and stood up from his crouching position. He threw the screwdriver into his backpack and dropped the hammer on the cave floor.

"We have to be careful that the door doesn't fall on us when we pry it open. Once I get the bolts out of the hinges, make sure you are out of the way because it might crash down. Okay?" Oz cautioned us. Our friend stooped down and rummaged through his backpack again until he pulled out a crowbar and a chisel. He zipped the bag up and tossed it farther back in the chasm away from the door. "Here we go," Oz warned us.

With the chisel in one hand titled at a slant against the top of the bolt, he repeatedly tapped at the base of the handle with the hammer. CLUNK, CLUNK, CLUNK, CLUNK. He removed one bolt at a time until he finished all four hinges.

"Okay, stand back!" Oz retreated quickly. He dropped the tools and grabbed the crowbar while keeping a watchful eye on the steel hatch. Our friend stuck the sharp end of the iron tool into the gap between the door and the frame. "UUUHHH," Oz grunted. The door moved an inch. Jimbo and I stood motionless while he attacked the project from a new angle. This time Oz held the crowbar horizontally about a foot above his head. He yanked the metal tool as the door slowly slanted toward us. Oz swiftly darted out of the way. CRREEAAAK, the heavy door fell to the stone floor. Suddenly, a few rats scurried past us. BOOM! A cloud of dust filled the corridor. For quite a few seconds I couldn't see my buddies, but with all the coughing, I knew they were near. The air leisurely cleared as the grime settled to the ground.

"You did it!" I peered into the darkness over Oz's shoulders.

"Right on!" Jimbo cheered.

Oz squinted into the beam of our flashlights and grinned proudly. His face was completely covered in dust. The door rested in its new place on the cave floor, allowing us to enter further into the mysterious unexplored passage!

# CHAPTER 15
## Unexpected Guests

L et's go in!" Jimbo shouted as he ran past Oz and stood at the entrance to the newly cleared passage. Oz seemed more concerned with gathering up the tools. He placed them in his backpack, swung it over his shoulder and readjusted his hardhat.

"I'm ready," Oz announced.

Our humble friend was rarely one to boast about his accomplishments. Nevertheless, I was again amazed by my buddy's ability to figure out and engineer solutions to problems using only limited tools or materials. We had Oz to thank. Jimbo, who was already walking ahead into the new chasm, and I together would never have gotten that door open. Oz and I remained to examine the heavy door. It was made out of a massive piece of metal, so weighty that the three of us could never lift it up.

Suddenly we heard our buddy let out a scream in the next passage: "ARGH!" The sound of his bare feet slapping the cave's floor became louder as he scampered back towards us. I froze. Even in the dim light, Jimbo's face was pale with fear and astonishment. "You won't believe this. There's a library back there with books, rats, and a skeleton of some dead guy sitting in a chair..." Jimbo went on describing the room but I couldn't hear anything he said after "a skeleton of some dead guy." His words sent chills down my spine. I snapped back to reality, remembering that he constantly played practical jokes on us.

"Yeah, right," I responded in disbelief.

"No, seriously, come and see for yourself!" Jimbo urged.

Having been the victim of my friend's pranks in the past, I ordered him to go first. Oz nodded in agreement. We both waited for Jimbo to enter the new threshold. Oz walked ahead of me, and I followed with an eerie feeling. I climbed on the metal door and jumped off the other side. The new corridor looked more like a manmade hallway than a cave. The walls were smooth. I trailed Oz as the light from his helmet brightened our route. The pathway led to another open portal.

On the opposite side of the doorway was a secret room. Its floors and walls were blanketed with block and brick patterns of mature stone tile. The room was long and narrow. Antique shelves overflowing with old books lined the entire wall. The stuffy smell of mold was overwhelming, and the area was covered with cobwebs and grime. Rodent droppings were everywhere. And there, in the far corner just as Jimbo had described, was what appeared to be a human carcass.

"A skeleton!" I shouted, frozen by the sight of its leathery skull.

A creepy numbness overwhelmed me. With empty eye sockets staring at us, the shriveled corpse was poised high and well postured in a wingback chair, cloaked in a dust encrusted, scarlet smoking jacket. A matching silk ascot draped the skeleton's bony neck, which remained paralyzed in the seat next to an old-fashioned kerosene lantern. As our flashlight beams moved about the room, the shadows bounced off the skull's eye sockets creating the illusion that the deceased was looking around at us. I knew my fears were irrational and that the corpse was not alive, but the whole experience gave me the jitters.

"Hey, there's a stairway over here!" Jimbo spoke as he advanced forward.

"Wait a minute," Oz urged him to slow down.

I agreed and begged my friend, "Wait Jimbo, this sure looks like a dead person to me. There might be something dangerous down here."

Jimbo didn't agree. "You can turn back if you're frightened, but I'm hunting for treasure. We're close, I can sense it."

My fear turned into rage at Jimbo's comment. "I'm not scared!"

"Okay let's climb these stairs then," Jimbo pushed me aside.

To prove a point, I shoved him out of my way and hurried ahead up the stone staircase. Counting more than forty steps and ascending into dark chasms which lead to a dead-end; I shined my flashlight down an unexplored passage.

"There's a roadblock at the end of these stairs," I hollered back at my friends who were lagging behind.

Three short steps at the end of the passageway lead to a blank wall. I slowly crept up to the top of the stairway to a wooden barrier. I knocked on the door with my flashlight.

"It sounds hollow. Do you think we'll be able to hack through here?" I asked Oz.

"I don't know. Hmm. Maybe we can push our way through it." Oz pressed his hands on yet another door.

He and I stood next to each other, forcing our body weight against the wooden barricade at the top of the steps. We felt the door dislodge a little bit.

"Let's push on a count of three. ONE, TWO...." I instructed Oz.

"THREE!" I shouted.

With all our strength Oz and I pushed our bodies up against the door. Jimbo continued to pull on a chain by the wall behind us. It made a loud echoing, CLANK!

Simultaneously, Jimbo asked, "What's this for?"

At that instant, I was airborne and free falling into the unknown. The timber blockade we were pushing against thrusted us forwards, and we traveled from our mysterious dark passage into the bright light of a formal dinner party. The wooden hatch slammed against a wall with a deafening, BOOM, followed by the sounds of clinking tableware and broken dishes smashing to the floor. Oz and I went plummeting headfirst onto a long lace table cloth.

"UGGGHHH," my stomach hit the hard edge of the backside of a dining room chair, which was positioned in front of the properly set table. My right hand landed fist first in the middle of a stuffed turkey, causing the bird to fly directly toward some of the blank stares of the guests. The forks, spoons, and knives that had been so precisely placed next to the porcelain china went sailing throughout the area. As the formally dressed people moved quickly to get out of the line of fire, the turkey landed in the lap of an elderly woman wearing a beaded purple dress. Horrified, she stood up and screamed as the buttery carcass plopped onto the floor.

Within seconds, Oz came crashing down into a two-tiered cake and landed next to me on the table knocking over a bottle of red wine and a bunch of flowers. The remaining guests were dodging food chunks and tableware as we made our abrupt, uninvited entrance. Frosting covered Oz's face. The revelers glared with shock and astonishment as they wiped their gowns and tuxedos off.

Luckily, neither one of us had collided with any of the dinner guests. There was still total silence. As I wondered how we could go from an innocent cave exploration, and end up crashing into somebody's dining room, my face began to burn with embarrassment. At that moment, I wanted to disappear into thin air.

"EXCUSE YOU!" A tall, thin gray-haired man broke the silence with his proper British accent. He had a long mustache that curled at each end of his face and a steamy look in his eyes. It was intimidating. His classy tuxedo shirt was covered with the splatter of red wine and a spray of gravy from when Oz and I crashed through the tunnel.

Jimbo stood confidently behind us at the entrance to the secret passage. He whistled and commented nonchalantly, "Hello in there. I guess we now know what this chain does."

"Who are you children? How dare you intrude on our dinner party?" The gray-haired man shouted red faced. His lower lip was shaking in frustration. I noticed Oz licking frosting from his fingertips. There was a cold unfriendliness in the old man's voice.

Oz announced: "Yummy, this butter cream frosting is delicious."

"I am going to call the police, you RAPSCALLIONS!" He yelled. The veins in his forehead were bulging out. We froze. Intimidated by the man in his formal black suit and tie, there was no question we were in a huge dilemma. From somewhere in the blur of people, who were now delicately chattering, I heard a familiar voice.

"Buzz, is that you?" A recognizable girl's tone inquired. I couldn't believe my eyes.

It was Stephanie Long, she was in my class last year!

"Stephanie, do you know these boys?" A slender platinum haired lady in a sparkly black dress stood up.

"These boys go to my school, Grandma." Stephanie gazed at me and smiled.

The lady was her grandmother! Stephanie's family must own this place that the secret passage from Turtle Cave led us to.

"I am going to call the police!" The angry man insisted. Mr. Long wiped his mustache with a linen napkin and stood up from the once elaborate dinner table.

"Just wait one moment, Rudolf." Stephanie's grandmother halted the angry man.

Standing up, I began to compose myself, placing the plates and some of the silverware back onto the table as carefully as possible. Oz was already standing between two of the formal guests. He had a square of butter stuck to the side of his head, and he still hadn't managed to lick all the frosting off his face.

"We discovered a cave by the shore that led us up here. I apologize that we fell into your formal gathering, Sir." I blurted out quickly. "But we exposed a maze of caverns and tunnels, and couldn't resist. We thought we'd find a treasure." I tried to convince the group.

"BOYS!" Nana shouted as she entered the dining room with both hands covering her cheeks. "I am in shock! What in the world are you doing here? Have you been following me? I am very disappointed in you. Look at the mess you have made!" She scolded, shaking her head in disbelief.

Nana sat down in a chair and exhaled deeply. She grabbed a napkin from the table and fanned herself. Jimbo, who was still standing in the cave chatting with two younger men in black suits, was the first to react. The men were fascinated by the secret passage behind the wall and stayed there examining it, while Jimbo jumped down and softly approached Nana. He tenderly put his arm around her shoulders and said:

"It's not as bad as it looks, Nana. We were exploring caves and came to this secret door; and look, we're just in time for dinner!" The guests laughed and Nana giggled, wiping her forehead with the napkin.

"You see Nana, we found this box when we were snorkeling. And then we discovered a drawing scratched in the lid of the box. I wanted to throw it away, but Buzz said 'keep it' so we checked local maps but couldn't find what we were looking for. Then we discovered the cave down the street from here, when we were surfing." Jimbo seemed to have calmed everyone down.

"Okay. See Rudolf? These young men are not burglars. You can find another white shirt upstairs in the back of your closet." Stephanie's grandmother spoke sternly. "Let's hear what else they have to say before we get too hasty." She insisted with a kind voice.

Realizing we had a chance to get out of trouble, I began to elaborate. "We were surfing when we found a cave near the cliffs that resembles a turtle's head. We started to explore the different passages until we found the one that led us here." I excitedly told the story of our adventure.

Occasionally, Jimbo or Oz would fill in with the particulars of our escapade. By now the entire gathering had assembled in the dining room behind the chair that Nana was sitting in. There were men and women and a couple of boys and girls besides Stephanie, who where dressed like miniature adults. Gasps of amazement filled the room as we crammed in the details of our adventure.

"We thought we'd find a pirate's treasure or something like that," I added, which prompted giggles from some of the dinner guests.

And then, Jimbo with his arm still around Nana's shoulders announced, "Oh yeah, there's a shriveled skeleton of some old man in a red shiny bathrobe down those stairs."

A few women shrieked. Nana looked at him in shock.

"A withered carcass, Rudolf, NOW, you may call the police!" Stephanie's grandmother commanded in a strident voice to the uptight man, who was just leaving the room.

Mrs. Long looked at us with a strange but forgiving expression as we were now huddled around Nana's chair. She studied us for a moment, regained her composure and gestured to a servant draped in a gingham apron. "Dinner will be served in the tea room, instead. I am so sorry for the inconvenience. It has been a very unusual evening." She sounded extremely calm, yet authoritative.

"I'll say," Nana interrupted.

Stephanie's grandmother continued, "Please follow Helen into the corridor, and Rudolf and I will join you shortly." The servant opened the large double doors that led to the next room, and most of the guests who were conversing excitedly among themselves followed her. Helen remained by the doorway and welcomed the party-goers into the tea room, while Nana, Stephanie, and her grandma waited in the dining room with us until the police arrived. I took another look at the table and wondered what food was still intact enough to eat. We sure had made an unforgivable mess. Maybe they would have to order pizza.

When the police arrived, Stephanie and her grandmother rejoined the guests in the tea room. We were asked to remain at the mansion while the investigation was going on. They still had many questions for us, and a homicide team even showed up to examine the skeleton.

Stephanie and her grandma served us some of the appetizers that we hadn't destroyed before returning to the party. We sat down at the table with Nana who was watching the operations of the police with fascination. While we were sampling what was left of the cake that Oz had landed on, a deputy sheriff in a khaki uniform interviewed us. Her name was Officer Chong. She inquired about the cave, the skeleton, and our journey through the passage. During the discussion our attention was constantly interrupted by official looking people walking in and out of the secret cavern. Some were in plain clothes, and others wore uniforms with heavy clanking utility belts. The coroner, a middle aged man with salt and pepper speckled hair, finally arrived wearing a white lab coat. Out of the crook of my eye, I noticed him crouch into the secret entrance from the dining room. When he exited the tunnel with a black plastic bag on the gurney, he caught everyone's attention. The coroner and his assistant rolled the gurney with the old corpse out of the cavern, and the wheels creaked like an unbalanced grocery cart as they strolled by us. We could hear the murmur and gasps of the party guests in the living room as their procession cleared the hallway and exited the mansion.

"Okay, the passage is secure." We were addressed by a tall blond man with a well groomed beard. He wore faded blue jeans and a denim shirt, with a badge attached to his snakeskin belt and introduced himself as the head detective in charge of the investigation.

"I'm Detective Kartner." He smiled at Officer Chong and thanked her, then turned to the three of us. The shoulder holster that contained his gun was quite intimidating. Jimbo, mesmerized by the object, reached out to touch it, but the detective admonished him.

"Never approach an officer's gun like that, Son," Detective Kartner commanded with authority.

Officer Chong flipped her notepad shut, stood up, and shook our hands.

"Goodbye boys, it was nice meeting you. Thank you for your cooperation." She smiled and left.

"I'd like you kids to show me how you got in here." Detective Kartner motioned us into the passage.

Nana nodded her approval and stayed seated in her chair. Jimbo entered first, then Oz. The detective and I followed. The police had mounted temporary lights in the bend of the corridor's ceiling during their investigation. The artificial lighting made it seem like daylight. The passage, which lead to the chamber where we discovered the shriveled corpse appeared unchanged and wasn't creepy to me anymore in the bright light. The chair where the skeleton rested was still in the exact same place. Detective Kartner held a massive black flashlight that looked like a nightstick. Walking in front of us, he was a very imposing figure and appeared even bigger under the low ceiling of the cavity. As we followed the detective through the chamber, two uniformed policemen and several of the men from the party caught up with our group. Fortunately, the angry man named Rudolf, who is Stephanie's grandfather was not among them. The party guests who joined us looked very out of place wearing their formal suits and ties with polished shoes in the cave. Occasionally, one of them would slip and lose their footing because of the slick soles on their shoes. One of them even fell on his butt. We couldn't help laughing. He didn't seem to care, as the men babbled amongst themselves in sheer amazement over our breakthrough.

"To think this was here all these years and we never knew about it," they kept repeating with bewilderment.

"Look," another man interjected in the hidden library, "most of these books are over one hundred years old!"

A few of the guests remained behind, fascinated by the library and the many publications that filled its shelves. We continued to track Oz's chalk marks, which lead the remainder of our motley group all the way back to the rope leading down to the sea cave. The youngest of the men, a stocky guy with jet black dreadlocks and a goatee, followed Detective Kartner and my friends down the rope. One of the police officers attached a hanging ladder that he retrieved from an emergency kit so that the rest of the guests could scale the ledge with ease. I could already hear the pounding of the tide rushing into the cave, indicating that the ocean was rising. From the entrance to the cavern, we could see there was still light from the afternoon sun. The entire group marveled at our extraordinary discovery. Jimbo, Oz and I were very proud and eager to unveil the story of our exploration of Turtle Cave. The younger man removed his tuxedo and swam in his underwear out of the cave's mouth to see the turtle shape at the peak of the cavern.

"Just wanted to witness it for myself," he reassured us. As he waded back in, the young man shouted, "Yeah! It's true, you boys weren't exaggerating. It gives the impression that the head of a giant turtle is sticking out of the top of the cave!" The young man began to chant: "TURTLE CAVE, TURTLE CAVE, TURTLE CAVE!" The rest of his group joined in, which they ended with a hoot.

When I asked the detective if he was going to swim out to see the turtle sculpture at the entrance he replied: "I'll take a rain check. We'll come back later in a police boat to investigate this case further."

After the chanting died down, the detective announced, "Okay folks, it's getting dark and the tide is moving in rapidly. Let's move along and get back to the mansion."

While we made our way back through the cavern to the mansion, Detective Kartner began to lecture us about the dangers of exploring unknown caves.

"This is a great discovery boys, but it is extremely hazardous. You were risking your lives goofing around down here." He scolded us in an authoritative voice.

Climbing up the emergency hanging ladder was easy. From the ledge, we headed to the library where we had found the corpse and then returned to the mansion's formal dining room through the secret passage. The trip seemed so short now. We carried our surfboards the whole way back to the house with help from the others in our group. I was the first to exit the secret passage and emerge into the dining room. Nana and Stephanie were sitting together. They smiled. Many of the dinner guests were still reveling in conversation watching our every move. As the last of the explorers returned from the cave, the partygoers swarmed around them wanting to know more. The young man who had jumped in the ocean got the most attention. The room was overflowing with enthusiasm about our tale. Some people were already planning their own explorations of the cave.

"I have been speaking with Stephanie and she tells me that she knows the three of you from school. And I guess you were in her class last year, Buzz." Nana said with a jolly chuckle. Feeling a little shy, I was at a loss for words. Stephanie looked pretty in her dress. Her brown eyes met mine and I got the same warm feeling that overcame me when I saw her in school. Stephanie's hair seemed different. She looked more like a lady with it rolled up on her head, and I felt short next to her because she was wearing fancy shoes with high heels.

"I'm ready to go." Detective Kartner interrupted my day dream. He shook each of our hands and then announced, "We have completed our initial investigation. Thank you for your teamwork. If we have any further questions, we will be in touch."

Nana got up from the chair that she had been sitting in the entire time, and said: "I'll drive you boys home. Your surfboards look like they will fit in the back seat of my car. We'll all cram into the front seat for the short ride home." Nana had regained her warm familiar smile. "Hmmm, exploring caves and searching for pirate's treasure is a natural thing for boys your age to do, I guess. That's what you children have been up to all of this time riding off with tools in your packs. I was starting to worry that it was something worse. Let's go out to the car," she directed.

Our trio followed Nana through the revelers and other onlookers who had arrived at the mansion. Apparently, word had gotten out around the neighborhood and men and women in beach attire were mixed in with the formal visitors in the main hallway. Everyone's gaze focused on our small troupe. With our backpacks over our shoulders and surfboards under our arms, we paraded through the mansion towards the front doorway. Jimbo and Oz followed my lead. We looked like exhausted travelers at the conclusion of a long journey. Not to mention, we were filthy from three trips through the cave system.

# CHAPTER 16
## Mystery Solved!

As we walked outside of the mansion, we were greeted by a fiery red sky with a glowing orange sunset. The front of the building was a familiar sight. We had ridden our bicycles and walked by it hundreds of times before. The four white pillars that adorned the façade of the dwelling had a pearly radiance, contrasting the brilliantly tinted sky that complimented the pink stucco walls of the old building. Across the street, the glassy evening ocean mirrored the last light of the day. It was late, and I had completely forgotten about the time. There was a generous assembly of curious onlookers jamming the street in front of the estate's exterior walls. Somehow, even the TV News found out about our adventure and arrived at the house to report on the story. We watched the evening broadcast on a monitor set up outside the mansion.

A male announcer appeared on the screen.

"AND NOW, OUR LOCAL TOP STORY," the gentleman spoke. "THREE BOYS STUMBLED INTO THE ENTRANCE OF A CAVE WHILE SURFING AT A LOCAL INLET. THE CAVERNOUS BLUFF LEADS TO A SECRET PASSAGE AND ENDS INSIDE ONE OF OUR NEIGHBORHOOD'S HISTORIC HOMES. ALTHOUGH THEY DIDN'T FIND THE TREASURE THEY HAD HOPED FOR, THE YOUNG MEN HAVE SOLVED THE EIGHTY-FIVE YEAR OLD MYSTERIOUS

DISAPPEARANCE OF THE NOTORIOUS SMUGGLER, KENNETH JOHN EDDINGTON, ORIGINAL BUILDER AND OWNER OF THE EDDINGTON HOUSE. NOW BACK TO CORRESPONDENT LACY LANE, LIVE AT THE LOCAL SCENE OF THIS MOST IMPRESSIVE DISCOVERY...LACY?"

The announcer squinted, and then the female correspondent appeared on the screen. As the reporter bombarded us with questions, the cameraman continued to focus his lens on us. Meanwhile, my parents were watching the exact same live broadcast at home. I was already two hours late for dinner. The reason we know how everything played out on television was because we later obtained an entire video copy of the story from the news station. To my embarrassment, my mom showed all of her friends and our relatives the piece. After seeing it over and over again, I have that moment stored in my head for life! It went something like this:

"Lacey Lane here live, with a discovery made by three young surfers. They actually discovered a cave while surfing, which led to a secret passage in this historic home." The camera panned and showed the front of the mansion.

Lacy Lane continued, "How did you discover the secret passage that leads into the mansion from the cave?"

Jimbo pushed his way in front of the camera and announced confidently into the microphone, "We were surfing here and we discovered this cave and explored it and found a skeleton. Then I pulled a rusty old chain to open the secret entrance into the dining room of this estate." Jimbo was calm and brazen.

On the other hand, I froze in front of the camera like an animal at night staring into the oncoming headlights of a car. Consumed with guilt, all I could think of was the lie I told my parents about being at the skate park, while we were exploring a dangerous and unknown cave.

The TV correspondent Lacey Lane pulled the microphone away from Jimbo and continued:

"We are now going to speak with the lady of the house. Mrs. Long, did you know about the secret passages in the mansion before today? What exactly can you tell us about the mysterious cavern?"

The camera turned to Stephanie's Grandma, who politely replied, "Well, I can't tell you much. My parents bought this estate before I was born. They said it was boarded up and had been abandoned for several years. The previous owner had just disappeared, and the building remained vacant until it was purchased at auction by my family. We were not aware that any secret passages existed. When I grew up here, there was a lot of talk about smugglers and secret routes, but until today we didn't actually know of any." She smiled and the camera panned back to the correspondent.

"This discovery was quite a surprise for the current owners of the historical Eddington mansion. I'm Lacey Lane, back to you in the studio."

Nana avoided the cameras and waited in the crowd for us to finish speaking to the TV people. We followed her to the car. She opened the driver's door and the rear passenger door. We piled our surfboards in the back seat and slid past the steering wheel on the long front seat of the jalopy. Everyone was silent during the short ride back to Nana's place.

She wished us a solemn, "good luck at home," as she walked into her house, looking exhausted.

My house was quiet when I finally arrived home behind schedule.

"Hi, I'm home. Sorry I'm a little late!" I casually apologized to my parents as I entered the living room. Instantly, I was bombarded with their cold, stoic glares at the doorway. Not really sure what I was in for, I got ready to tell my parents, full of enthusiasm about our adventure:

"Hey Mom, Dad, you will never believe what happened today!"

"WE KNOW!" My father snapped at me. "Where did you tell your mother you were going today?"

In one instant my elation changed into a feeling of having a lump of frigid iron pushed down in my stomach.

"We changed our plans?" I tried to recover, but my response was weak.

Regardless of all the excitement involving the cave and its mystery, I had let my parents down. I lied. They trusted me and I had disappointed them. Now I seriously regretted my actions, realizing what I had done. My greed and the prospect of getting rich by finding someone else's treasure misdirected me.

"Go wash up and eat your supper," My mother commanded sternly.

After I sat down at the dinner table, my father continued. "You assured us you'd be skateboarding at the skate park. Instead you were risking your life climbing around in dangerous ocean caves. If there had been a collapse, we never would have found you or your friends. What if you had ended up like that old skeleton?"

My father remained unsympathetic as he shot a look of disgust at me. He proceeded to lecture me as I sat picking at my cold plate of food. Occasionally, I could feel tears welling up in my eyes, but I controlled them. As my dad yelled mercilessly, my mother positioned herself behind him with her arms folded. She wore a very displeased look on her face which made me feel even more ashamed.

Just then, the phone in the kitchen rang. My mother picked it up.

"Oh, hello," she answered in a composed manner. I could hear every word. "Yes, Mrs. Gonzales. I had no idea either, and I am enormously disturbed as well!" It was clear that my mom was talking to Oz's mother. "Hold on one moment please, I'm going to switch telephones." My mother handed the receiver to my father and stormed out of the living room. "Okay you can hang up now."

My dad hung up the telephone and continued to rant unrelentingly. "We give you an extraordinary amount of freedom for a boy your age. We allow you to surf with your friends, and in return, we expect you to follow the rules. Not only were you untruthful, but you risked your lives to surf in a place with a rocky reef and no lifeguards!"

That night my dad also reminded me that a true Grommet is always honest and genuine. Grommets never lack integrity, and certainly don't tell lies. I remember his last words as he left me alone with my dinner. "Buzz, you'd better have respect for the ocean and the truth." As my father finished scolding me, he stomped into the parlor where my mother remained.

The chill in the kitchen was worse than my cold stew, and the meat tasted like rubber. The knot that had now formed in my throat made the meal even more unpleasant. I wanted to be a "true" Grommet, and I was ready to accept my punishment.

After about ten unbearable minutes of hearing muffled whispers from the living room, my parents returned and imposed their sentence: "We've spoken to Oz and Jimbo's parents and we agreed that you will all be grounded with six days of chores!" My mother announced and left the room.

"You are lucky that the woman who owns the house you broke into doesn't want the police to press charges. I don't know why. From what I heard you really did a lot of damage, even ruining the turkey, cake and an expensive bottle of red wine. Boy, how you charmed your way out of this exploit I don't know; but one thing is for sure, you will not be able to persuade your way out of the dog house here. And let me tell you mister, if anything like this happens again it will be the end of your friendship with Jimbo and Oz. Remember that! If the three of you had been doing anything criminal, instead of just exploring caves, your friendship with them would be over already. Do you get that?" My father's eyes were bulging out of their sockets.

"Yes sir, I get it," I answered.

Red faced, my dad continued with his tirade. "You will report to James' house tomorrow morning at seven o'clock, where his mother will put you to work for two days. The following two days, you will report to Oscar's mother for chores, and finally, the last several days will be spent here. We have plenty of things for you and your buddies to paint, clean, scrub, brush, trim and chop."

At that point I resigned myself to my penalty. The worst component was that my mom gave me the silent treatment, and refused to speak to me for six days. She wrote notes to me on little yellow sticky papers for everything. Our punishment seemed to last as if it were an eternity. After lunch on the sixth day, my mom approached us and alleviated us from our sentence. She finally broke her silence and softened, "You've done enough for now, I hope you boys have learned your lesson."

She gave me a tight hug and I really didn't want to leave her at that moment, but my friends urged me to go surfing with them. It was an easy sell. After being out of the ocean for almost a week, it felt gratifying to be back in the lineup. The waves were only knee to waist high and the afternoon wind made the water surface choppy. The sky was blue and the sun was warm. The surf wasn't spectacular, but that didn't bother me one bit. My first wave gave me a quick right wall that I raced across before I turned and jumped over the breaker like it was a ramp. I was proud to land on my feet on the other side of the little roller and was able to gracefully lie back down on my surfboard. I relaxed on the deck, and began the short paddle back to my friends. We sat on our boards waiting for the next set of waves.

I thought out loud, "Boy, this sure beats all of the hard work we have been doing over the past week."

"Yeah instead of finding a treasure, we found a lot of trouble," Oz grinned. "Next time you find a secret chest in the water, do me a favor and throw it back!" He added.

All three of us howled at that comment. Our attention was instantly diverted when another set of waves approached. Jimbo caught the first wave of the set. Oz wasn't in the right spot so he stopped paddling and turned his board back and rejoined us outside. Meanwhile, Jimbo popped up onto his feet and began slashing short little turns. Now, Oz was in perfect position for the next breaker. He caught it and shredded. Left alone, I was able to catch the next one. It was fast, and the thrill of the juicy little wave gave me that familiar feeling that I love so much about surfing. I felt like I was flying. We spent another hour in the water until it seemed that the waves were just not consistent anymore. Still dripping wet, we sat on the steps at the top of Main Beach and overlooked the sandy strip below.

"School starts next week." Jimbo could have just as well have stabbed me in the heart with his comment.

"Is summer over already? I can't believe it!" I groaned. The timer on my watch said there were only five days left!

"At least our school has a surf team. Tryouts are the last weekend in September, I heard." Jimbo eagerly reported.

"School's only four days away!" I exclaimed.

"Surf team could be fun, but we should get in better shape," Oz advised flexing his biceps.

"Yeah, we should GO FOR IT!" I suddenly was excited about the prospect of going back to school and joining the surf team. After all, my friends would be there too.

# CHAPTER 17
## The Final Reward

Sure enough, the first day of school came before I knew it. Somehow I lost my enthusiasm. The feeling of stiff new leather shoes on my feet felt constricting. New clothes, new text books and notebooks, pencils and pens all felt unfamiliar and reminded me of the homework I was going to be doing. Stephanie Long was in my class again, but Jimbo and Oz were in different classes. My teacher was Mrs.Toklas. She is nice, but it was real hard adjusting to the daily grind and not surfing every day.

The first big assembly was on the second day of school. All the classes for each grade level were led into the auditorium. My group was the last to be brought in. Scanning the huge hall I could see Jimbo and Oz were already seated with their classes in different rows. I didn't know why my stomach felt like there were butterflies in it. We were led to a row near the front. I waved to Oz who nodded. Jimbo, who was lost in conversation with the kid sitting next to him didn't see me waving. My class filled two rows. When we were told to stop, I sat down in my seat and focused my attention to the stage. The maroon curtains that draped the sides looked immense. Mrs. Toklas and the other teachers sat in the front row.

Our principal, Mr. Battle, walked from the left side to the podium at the center of the stage. The microphone whined with feedback as he leaned forward to speak into it. He grimaced and then smiled at the student who was operating the soundboard in the projection room in the back.

"Welcome students, please stand and recite the Pledge of Allegiance." He said as the color guard carried the flags onto the stage.

After the Pledge, we sat down and Mr. Battle cleared his throat and spoke into the microphone: "We will proceed with the assembly in just a moment. There are a lot of exciting events planned for this school year that we will talk about. But, first I would like to ask our local historian and social studies teacher Mr. Schimmel to come to the podium and make his presentation." Mr. Battle started clapping and soon the entire auditorium followed his example.

Mr. Schimmel, a small-framed, bald, middle aged man with a gray beard and small round spectacles approached the stage and shook our principal's hand. They stood there for a few seconds greeting each other. Finally, Mr. Battle swaggered off the stage while Mr. Schimmel pulled some papers out of his blazer pocket and shuffled them on the podium.

"Eh-hemmm, good morning students." Mr. Schimmel's voice was high pitched and sounded a little squeaky. "I am here to tell you about some local history. About 80 years ago, before anyone in this room was even born, a man named Kenneth John Eddington was a prominent and wealthy member of our town's high society. Apparently, he used to throw some really big balls back then." There was a roar of laughter. He looked up and didn't seem to understand why, but then Mr. Schimmel smiled and continued his lecture, "Mr. Eddington lived in a mansion close to the cliffs in an older section of town. During the prohibition period when liquor was illegal, many fortunes were made smuggling booze ashore in the area. The smugglers would use beach caves to hide their wares. Mr. Eddington vanished suddenly and without a trace. A reward was offered by the local bank, but until recently no one knew what became of Mr. Eddington."

After Mr. Schimmel's presentation, Jimbo, Oz, and I, were called to the stage. Mr. Schimmel continued as we stood side by side facing the audience: "These three students have uncovered two important mysteries. The first was how and where the smugglers were getting their loot safely to shore. For many years law enforcement were baffled by the constant flow of liquor during Prohibition, a time when it was illegal to have even a nice bottle of wine in your home. These three young men solved that puzzle this past summer when they discovered the secret hidden cave system that the smugglers used to haul their barrels. The liquor was safely smuggled through the Eddington Mansion during the Prohibition period. Mr. Eddington was a highly respected member of the community and you might say that he was above the law and suspicion. Of course there were rumors. Anyways...," He paused for a moment and looked at the three of us on stage.

I stood embarrassed in front of a sea of faces with the bright lights of the stage shining in my eyes. Despite that, far in the back row I could see Bradly Booker's angry face. Looking to my right, Oz stood at attention. Jimbo, on the other hand seemed to be enjoying himself. He was clowning around in front of the whole school, nodding with his arms holding on to an imaginary podium mimicking Mr. Schimmel, while he spoke. I chuckled as my friend's antics put me at ease. Oz broke his silence and burst out with laughter too. The rest of the big hall followed laughing and shouting. Pandemonium broke out. Even Mr. Schimmel looked at Jimbo, nodded, and grinned. Mr. Battle returned to the stage motioning with both of his arms raised over his head for the students to calm down. He shot Jimbo a warning look and waved his index finger at him. Peace and quiet soon returned to the auditorium.

Mr. Schimmel continued. "So what actually happened to good Mr. Eddington? Well, that is the second mystery I will be speaking about. Many theories filled the newspapers and the story even made national news. Some thought he was murdered. Others thought he ran off with his mistress. But these three fellow students finally put all those rumors to rest."

Mr. Schimmel chuckled and momentarily took his attention off our trio. He pointed at Stephanie Long in the audience motioning for her to rise. "I guess he was living at your grandparents' house all these years. Please stand up, young lady." Stephanie stood up slowly and rapidly retreated to her seat a second later. "History is fascinating. I think that you must all feel the same." A faint murmur echoed through the auditorium. "Miss Long has a unique connection to this historical mystery. Her grandparents now own the old Eddington estate. It seems that Mr. Eddington went into his hidden library one day and had a stroke or a heart attack and died. The secret chamber was so well hidden that no one ever found the body until your fellow students stumbled upon it looking for pirate's treasure." More giggles were heard from the crowd. "Now, I have the pleasure of introducing Mr. Smith from the local bank. It appears that he has a connection to this mystery, too." Just then, we saw the principal's secretary walking my mom, and Jimbo and Oz's mothers down the side aisle towards the stage.

"What's gong on, now?" I thought.

Mr. Schimmel stepped aside as our principal returned onstage with a tall silver haired man in a dark three piece suit. He looked as old as the skeleton we recently discovered in the cave. The man appeared gigantic compared to everyone next to him as he leaned over to speak into the microphone which was attached to the podium.

"Well good morning children. Let me introduce myself. My name is Mr. Smith, President of Main Beach Bank, here on behalf of your local Savings and Loan. As you all know, we're conveniently located in town across from City Hall. If any of you haven't opened savings accounts, ask your parents or guardians to bring you down to the bank and we'll set you up with your own savings book. Your piggy bank won't pay you interest. Haha." Mr. Smith seemed to be the only one laughing at his joke. Mr. Battle and Mr. Schimmel nodded and smiled approvingly as he spoke. "Now, I have the pleasure of honoring these three young men with an eighty year old reward for finding Mr. Eddington and solving this long overdue mystery."

"REWARD!" Oz, Jimbo and I looked at each other and repeated his last word in unison.

Mr. Smith stood up straight momentarily, as if to stretch his back and then hunched over to speak. "After the disappearance of Mr. Eddington, his family placed a reward in trust with our bank. The reward has grown substantially in the many years since it was deposited into the bank. Ah, the power of compound interest is magnificent!" Mr. Smith motioned to our mothers to come up on stage. Our principal led them toward us. My mom walked up to me and put her hand on my shoulder with a proud smile.

Returning to his speaking position, Mr. Smith announced: "I am administering equal reward checks to the mothers of these young men for putting an end to this mystery. Thank you."

The entire auditorium applauded as we were led off the stage. The rest of the assembly was a blur, and school ended when the gathering finally concluded.

Before we left the building Oz came over to me and Jimbo and asked, "Do you Grommets want to surf this afternoon?" I looked at Mom. She nodded approvingly.

"Meet you at the shack in an hour!" I waved to my friends.

We sure didn't discover gold and jewels and treasure in the cave as we had imagined, nor did we find the waves we were hoping for that afternoon. Instead, our small fortune found us in the form of a reward from the local bank. In the end, our parents allowed us each to buy one new surfboard and wetsuit. We had to put the rest of the money into a savings account for college.

The sea was flat like a pancake. Oz, Jimbo, and I sat on the velvety sand gazing at the pelicans bobbing on the serene ocean. We reminisced about our summer adventures while our trio exhausted the rest of the afternoon daydreaming aloud about our future careers as professional surfers.

'GO FOR IT' became my new creed as I remembered the physical strength, endurance, and quick thinking I encountered during the summer months I became a real Grommet. I may not have grown much in size, but my confidence certainly emerged. Our surfing adventures, rescuing Nana, climbing the rope, discovering Turtle Cave, and solving a long overdue mystery were just some of the accomplishments I attributed to my new self image. Besides, joining the school surf team and winning contests could lead to bigger and better opportunities!

930121

Made in the USA